D1440743

Mustang

THOMAS C. HINKLE

Mustang

A Horse of the Old West

FAMOUS
HORSE
STORIES

GROSSET & DUNLAP

Publishers, New York

¿H592mu

To
Little Thayer
and
Peter Whiteside

Mustang

I

IT was a fine spring day in the cattle country of the Old West. Big Bay, the mother of Mustang, a two-month-old colt, walked along a trail that led up a steep slope toward a line of rocky cliffs beyond. Three old worn-out range horses walked behind Big Bay and Mustang.

Big Bay had raised a number of colts. She was the kind of mother that watched for enemies and she was an unusual old mare in that she would fight for her colt. She would fight a wolf or a mountain lion, and once she had kicked a grizzly bear so quickly and so hard on his jaw that the grizzly was knocked back and Big Bay got away with her foal.

That had been two years ago. She had a new colt now—this small prancing one that seemed to be so full of life he couldn't stand still.

She was an unusually big mare, weighing over twelve hundred pounds. She was tall, rangy, quick on her feet and quick to see her enemies as a rule, although at this time she was moving toward a dangerous one that she could not see, and unfortunately there was no wind to help her scent him. He was a big mountain lion crouched flat on a high rocky ledge just above the horse and cattle trail that passed right beneath him.

Big Bay was not supposed to be way out here in the wild places, miles from the Horseshoe Ranch where she belonged. She had strayed away from the Horseshoe Ranch three days before with her little colt, Mustang, and before noon of that day Sam Mc-Swain had missed her. Sam, a foreman of the ranch, was a young man of only nineteen, but he had native ability for his job. He was next to the head foreman, Jim Parkman, on the vast Horseshoe Ranch. And both Sam and Jim owned cattle in their own right. Fortunately for Sam, he was now the owner of Big Bay and Mustang.

The colt had been born in a stable on the Horseshoe Ranch and Sam had petted him so much that at two months old he had learned to know Sam from all the other cowboys. Tall, raw-boned Jim Parkman had said one day to Sam, "If you keep on fooling with that colt, Sam, you'll have him so daggone full of tricks you'll plumb spoil him. Why, he's got so now that we can't throw a hat on the ground but what *he* carries it away!" And that was so. Mustang, to Sam's delight, would come up when Sam was seated on the ground, and if Sam would seem to pay no attention to him, he would pull Sam's hat off. Once when Mustang did this Sam had said to the other cowboys looking on, "This little colt is unusual. He'll make a great horse some day." "A great nuisance, maybe!" Jim had said, but Sam only laughed.

And so while Sam rode and hunted in the wild places now for Big Bay and her fine little foal, he had all these thoughts about the colt. Out here in these days, when a cowboy like Sam got to liking a horse like that, that horse seemed like a true human friend.

Sam had his field glasses, and now and then he would put his "lookers," as the cowboys called them, to his eyes and scan the countryside. As yet, he had seen no sign of Big Bay and Mustang.

If, at this minute, he had known what was happening across a high ridge beyond him, one that he couldn't see over, he would have started his horse running toward that place with all his might and Sam would have started shooting his rifle to scare that "mountain cat," as the cowboys called mountain lions. But, as it was, the big cat lay on the ledge, his mouth watering for that little colt prancing along beside his mother, coming nearer and nearer all the time.

Sam was in a dip between two high ridges and he started his horse up the farther slope. It was a high ridge and it was not far from that rocky ledge where the big crouching cat lay waiting.

Sam rode out of a cut in the ridge and came out in the open where all at once he saw one of the strangest fights in the Old West. As he rode into the open he saw the mountain lion leap, apparently for Mustang. But a strange thing happened to the big cat as he jumped. There was earth and loose shale rock on the ledge where he crouched and the lion's hind claws slipped as he leaped. Sam saw the place later. The result was that the big cat missed Mustang wholly and fell right under the front hoofs of Big Bay. On the instant Sam saw one of her hoofs strike down. She struck the beast fair in the head. She uttered a wild shriek and rained blows upon him with her front hoofs.

Then Sam saw Big Bay's head shoot down and he saw her gleaming teeth as she grabbed the big cat by the neck and tried to shake it as a dog would shake a rat.

Astonished and delighted with what he had seen, Sam rode up at a run. Big Bay was now pounding the dead beast with her front hoofs. She seemed wild with fear and rage. Sam saw one ugly cut on Big Bay's shoulder where a claw of the lion had cut as the beast leaped down, and there was Mustang standing quivering but unhurt. Sam uttered an exclamation of awe and joy. He dismounted and affectionately patted the trembling but now unafraid Big Bay. He said to Mustang, "Say, little feller, you're about the luckiest little colt that ever was! And if you are half the fighter that your mammy is you'll be a great horse!"

Mustang unhesitatingly came up close to Sam and Sam patted his shoulders and rubbed the hair smooth down his back. From the day Mustang had been born Sam had paid this

attention to him. One of the chief reasons
Sam was interested in this colt was because
of Big Bay. She was the most beautiful horse
on the ranch and she had, besides, unusual
intelligence and a fighting spirit.

Sam looked at her now and he talked to
her as he patted her on the neck. Even
though she sometimes wandered away from
the ranch if she was loose, she would come
up to any of the men she knew when they
dismounted and talked to her. Jim Parkman,
Charley Malone, Bud Allen, and all the men
at the ranch had a great liking for Big Bay.
While Sam talked to her he tied his lariat
rope around her neck and said, "Big Bay,
you're the greatest horse on the ranch, but
you must stay at home with Mustang or the
next mountain cat will get him. If it's not a
mountain cat it might be a wolf maybe. Too
much danger out here for this little feller
even with you to watch him."

The wind that blows so frequently in the
West lifted Big Bay's long foretop and blew

it to one side and her long flowing tail moved
steadily in the breeze. Big Bay quit trembling. She put her nose down toward the big
mountain lion, her eyes opened wide and she
snorted, but Sam reassured her and she
looked off in the distance. Presently she
made an unusual sound that caused Sam to
look at her eyes and he saw she was watching something in the distance. At first he
could see nothing but some buzzards far
away circling in the sky. But in a moment he
was aware that Big Bay saw something that
she was more concerned with than the circling buzzards. Sam saw the top of a horseman's head in the distance. The man was
riding in a low place on a rolling plain. Sam
mounted his horse and saw a small cloud of
dust, and then all at once he saw not one but
three horsemen galloping along in his direction.

As the horsemen came nearer, Sam saw
that they were his three friends, Jim Parkman, the ranch head foreman, Charley Ma-

lone and Bud Allen. The three cowboys rode up at a gallop and pulled their horses to a stand. When Sam told them what had happened they looked at the dead mountain lion, then looked at Big Bay with something in their eyes that showed how much they admired her. They dismounted, rubbed Big Bay, and praised her in their typical language, and grinned with admiration while they talked.

"Now *ain't* Big Bay the daggondest, fightingest horse!"

"You bet she is. She's plumb sour on mountain cats!"

"It's so, and if she was hungry enough she'd likely eat one for breakfast."

"I expect when she was a-stomping this cat she was a-thinking, 'Why daggone your hide! The *idee*—you a-trying to kill my little feller! I ain't got *no* use for you! You can't travel in my set—you're that disgusting!'"

"Yes, and likely she thought while she

stomped him, 'I suppose I *ought* to leave enough of you for the buzzards to pick on account they'll be hungry. Well, I'll mix 'em up a good mess of hash for once. I'll pound you up like a tough beefsteak. The buzzards is nice and I'll fix 'em a right nice meal.' "

As they talked they thought of how much she and Mustang meant to Sam. A month before the chief owner of the ranch had sold a herd of horses to be shipped into Kansas and Sam had bought Big Bay and Mustang, paying a higher price for them than for horses in general. But Jim and Charley and Bud knew. As they put it, "Sam was plumb set on these two from the first."

This was the last day of the spring round-up on the Horseshoe, one of the biggest cattle and horse ranches of the Old West. All the spring colts and calves, or any others that had not been found the spring before, were being rounded up to be branded. Already more than a score of riders were starting the horses toward the place for branding, and as the men looked toward the north they saw a large herd of horses gallop in the direction of the ranch with many riders behind them, "fogging them on."

Sam said, "Jim, you fellers go on. I'll ride slow like because I want to lead Big Bay. I don't want her to get loose again with Mustang." And at this Jim and Charley and Bud rode away. They sat as straight as posts in their saddles, with the easy grace of men who had grown up in the saddle—men who were among the best riders in the world.

Suddenly Jim Parkman's horse leaped quickly aside when a jack rabbit jumped up almost under his feet, but Jim, like a bird that knows its wings, was not moved from his saddle but swerved with the horse as if he had been a part of him. All these riding men here took all this the same as when a bird wheels and darts but keeps its balance. No one thought of it as anything unusual except, now and then, an Easterner, like the man one day who saw Jim and Sam ride.

The Easterner said, "Seems to me like the Maker of these men must be kinda proud Himself that He made them!"

In the meantime Sam was trotting his horse along at an easy pace, leading Big Bay, with Mustang galloping ahead, only sometimes the colt would "cut loose," kick up his heels and run off in the wrong direction. But Sam only grinned when he saw Mustang "letting out the kinks," as the cowboys would say, and he kept on grinning when Mustang would come tearing back like a thunderbolt and snort as he ran up close. Sam, the trained horseman, *knew* Mustang was an unusual colt! His actions on this day made Sam know it all the more. Mustang started out and ran as fast as any of the grown horses, which the colts at his age could do. Mustang "put on the brakes" as he raced ahead and snorted at nothing in particular. Back he came, running toward Sam and Big Bay as if he were scared stiff, but Sam understood. He said, as Mustang again, stiff legged, stopped himself almost under the nose of Sam's horse, "Mustang, if you grow up you're going to make a great horse. And I aim to keep close watch on you and keep you at the ranch. I can tell right now that you're like your old mammy—you got fight in you. You won't fight *me* but if animals or fellers ever get rough with you they'll think some kind of a mountain cat is all over 'em! I'm going to take your old fighting mammy here and tie her to a tree while we finish with this roundup of the horses. I won't let her loose again. She must stay at the ranch so I can know *you'll* grow up!"

When night fell, Sam tied Big Bay to a tree a little back from the campfire. After supper Sam and Mustang put on their usual show for the other men. Sam would scratch Mustang's neck for a while and Mustang would stand with his head low and his eyes half closed, telling plainly enough he liked to have Sam do this. Then Sam would grin broadly and he'd reach his arm over Mustang and tickle him under his flank and Mustang would kick. The reason the men enjoyed this so much was that Mustang seemed to *want* Sam to tickle him, for after Sam would scratch his neck for a time, Mustang would throw his head up and look a little wild in the eyes and crowd close to Sam. Sam knew what that meant. It meant that Mustang was saying, "Tickle me, Sam, I want to buck!" And Sam obliged him. There were other things Mustang would do that amused the men. Mustang had learned to pick up Sam's big hat from the ground and he would shake it a little, drop it and look at it with curiosity. It had happened one day after Sam had played with Mustang for a time that Sam thought he'd lie down and doze a little, putting his big hat over his face as the cowboys did when asleep on the plains. Mustang had come over and pulled

Sam's hat from his face and waked him up. After that Mustang could be counted on to do such things.

On this night the men, in due time, rolled up in their blankets, Sam with them, and they were soon all sound asleep.

It was a bright starlight night. The campfire cast its light on the cowboys, rolled up in their blankets and lying asleep with their feet toward the fire. The cowboys lay silent with their big hats over their faces. Standing in the shadows and looking curiously at sleeping Sam was Mustang. He walked up and stood with his nose less than a foot from the big hat over Sam's face. Big Bay was standing tied to the tree and she was about asleep. She knew, though, that Mustang was nosing around Sam over there. Well, she'd let him. In fact she'd be glad to let Sam take some of the care of him because she had never had a colt like Mustang, who seemed to be always awake and prancing around the

men. Sam was such a good sleeper that he
snored a little when he slept, as he was doing
now. Mustang heard the queer sounds coming from Sam and he must have wondered
what made Sam do it! In any case he must
have wondered something because he reached
down and, with his mouth, jerked Sam's hat
from his face. Sam, startled, sat up so quickly
that Mustang jumped back with a snort, but
he stood close, head down, looking at Sam.
This awakened Jim and Bud. When they
saw that it was Mustang with his pranks that
had awakened them, Jim said, "Sam, you'll
plumb spoil that colt, you always playing
with him. You better take Big Bay about a
mile away and tell her to keep him with her
so us fellers can sleep!"

Sam got up and, in his sock feet, led Big
Bay to another tree farther away. Mustang
came right along and when Sam had tied Big
Bay he spanked Mustang lightly on the
rump and said, "Daggone your little hide.

You stay here and be quiet and let us fellers sleep!"

But Mustang didn't go to sleep. He only stood there and looked at Sam walking back toward the small campfire.

II

MUSTANG was nine months old when an accident befell Big Bay that took her from him. Sam McSwain had put oats in her feed box that morning and scratched her neck and talked to her as he always did before riding away for the day. He talked to her as if she could understand, saying, "Now I'll see you and Mustang tonight when you come in for your oats."

The day passed. It was sunset when Sam and Jim Parkman rode in together. The other men had already come in. Sam had just started to dismount when, looking out on the plain, he said, "Well! Look there. There's

Big Bay and there's something the matter with her. She can't walk straight."

Big Bay came on. She reached the ranch yard and fell. The men gathered around her. There was a great swelling on her jaw and every man understood. Jim said, "Snake bite! A daggoned rattler got her."

And it was true. Big Bay had watched carefully all her life, but while she was eating in some tall green grass that morning a big rattler had struck without warning.

The men stayed up with her until morning and did all they could, but at sunrise this splendid fighting mother was gone.

Sam said to Mustang who was standing near, "Well, little feller, she's gone but you're coming right along. We'll look after you."

Several days passed. Mustang was kept on a long rope near the ranch house so that he could eat grass and get his exercise. And then an interesting thing happened. Old Bill, a range horse that was getting on in years, grazed around close to Mustang, and the cook at the ranch said, "Old Bill won't leave Mustang. He stays right around him all day."

A week of this had passed when Jim said, "Sam, turn Mustang loose with Old Bill. Old Bill never goes far and he always comes in at night for his oats. Let Mustang grow up natural like."

This was done, and it turned out as Jim had said. Old Bill never went more than a few miles from the ranch and for some time Sam kept a close watch to see how this friendship would come out. But each day he was more convinced that all was well. Sometimes in the afternoon he would see Old Bill and Mustang standing close together like two old horses that have long been together and like each other's company. Each night Old Bill would come in, and each night Mustang came in with him to spend the night in the stable.

And so it was that Mustang grew and

lived for four and a half years on the Horse-shoe Ranch. By this time all the men in a wide territory knew of Mustang. He was now a great, bright bay horse with four white stocking legs and a white mark on his chest that reached in a narrow line to his right shoulder where it ended in a rounded spot. He was as devoted to Sam McSwain as a dog might be devoted to a man. Although Jim Parkman had once said, "Sam, you'll plumb spoil that colt," he and all the other men had long ago changed their minds about that.

Four and a half years are but a little time in the life of a man, but it is a long time in the life of a horse. When a horse is four and a half years old, almost half of the best part of his life has been lived. Mustang, however, was considered still too young to undergo hard riding. Sam had him broken to the saddle and Mustang was so big and so tall and strong for his age that Sam had ridden him about, here and there, for some time.

But he wanted Mustang to be at least five years old before he rode him as he would any of the older horses. At five years Mustang would be ready.

Jim and Sam now owned a controlling interest in the Horseshoe Ranch and these two proved how kind and thoughtful they were in regard to horses when they turned every range horse loose when he got old, so that he could come and go as he pleased. Mustang, up to this spring, had grazed on the range with these old horses that had been retired. But he and Old Bill were still special friends. These two were generally seen together on the range and they seldom went more than a few miles from the ranch house during the long summer days.

Mustang had been so much petted by Sam and Jim and Charley and all the other men that there was never a doubt in their minds but that he would come home in a day or two no matter how far out on the range he chose to go. And Mustang had Sam's brand on him so that he was safe so far as all the other ranch owners were concerned.

One evening Mustang and Old Bill came galloping into the ranch yard together. The men had all come in from the range and were out near the stables. Old Bill performed his usual action. Arrived at the place, he snorted loudly and, with head and tail high, he trotted clear around one of the corrals, came up close to Sam and, looking off toward the west, snorted as if he were scared by something. But the men all knew that Old Bill wasn't scared. Sam knew him best of all. He came up and scratched Old Bill's neck while he stood looking off across the plains toward the skyline, but Old Bill was not paying any attention to the place beyond him. He was only acting. He acted as if he hardly knew that Sam was scratching his neck, yet that was all he wanted. Jim came up and began to rub Old Bill on the flank, at the same time telling him he was still one of the best of horses. Jim said proudly, "Bill, you always

had sense. You got as much sense as a feller!"

Mustang in the meantime was rubbing his
nose on Sam's shoulder and he began to nose
around Sam's shirt. Sam then scratched Mustang's neck as he said, "Here you are again.
You want your neck scratched, too. You and
Old Bill are different from the others. You
both want your oats now and you will get
'em, too, plenty!"

Presently Sam went into the stable and put
oats in the feed boxes and the two horses stood
side by side eating.

Very early the next morning, both being
free, they started off across the plain together
and they were feeling so good that they both
kicked up their heels and snorted as they galloped away. They did this before any of the
men were up except the old cowboy cook,
Buck Jenkins. Buck saw the two playing and
running across the prairie in the first streaks
of the dawn, but he thought nothing of it as
he had seen them do this many times before

and they both had always come back, Mustang as a rule running in ahead of Old Bill. It never occurred to Sam or Jim or any of the men that anything might happen to Mustang during these summer months. He was now a tall, rangy young horse and it was known that he had great speed. He had shown these men that he had only to play at running to outrun any horse they had ever seen him run with on the ranch.

If he had got out in the winter they would have been alarmed because he might have been in danger of the big gray wolves on the range, but these beasts never tackled big horses in the summer months. It was the young cows that they set upon. And anyway, up to now both Old Bill and Mustang, as already mentioned, never went far.

So it was that no one thought anything about Mustang running away that morning with Old Bill. However, when several days had gone by and one evening Old Bill came in alone, Sam was a little concerned. He thought he would soon see Mustang coming across the prairie, running like the wind for the ranch. But he didn't come. Sam gave Old Bill his oats as usual that evening and also put some in Mustang's feed box. A little later it was suppertime and all the men went in the house to eat—all but Sam. After Buck had called that supper was ready, Jim said, when he saw Sam was not coming, "Come on and eat, Sam. Mustang will come. He'll be here by the time we get through supper."

Sam said, "You go on and eat, Jim. I'll come in before long."

The men went in the house and Sam stood out in the yard looking out across the plains toward the west where Old Bill had come from. The time went on and Sam kept looking and hoping that any minute he would see his big bay horse with the white stocking legs thundering across the plains for home. Sam certainly wanted to see this.

After a time Sam said to himself as he looked across the prairie, "Now why don't he

come in?" And then affectionately, "Daggone his hide. I don't see why he has done
this." Sam had reason for being a little concerned since this was the *first* time that Old
Bill had ever come in without Mustang.

Sam still kept on looking and hoping, but
all at once the dark began to come and no
matter how hard Sam looked for his much-
loved big bay horse all that could be seen
was the plain stretching away to the darken-
ing skyline, and to Sam that skyline didn't
look as it used to—it just looked awful lone-
some. All that night he kept telling himself
that maybe everything would be all right—
that when he would wake up and go to the
stable the next morning, there would be Mustang big as life, waiting to have his neck
scratched. But no matter how much Sam
tried to make himself think this, he couldn't
be satisfied. And although that night Jim and
Bud Allen said Mustang would come in, and
although all the other men went to sleep,
Sam lay awake. He lay awake and listened

for the sounds of a galloping horse's hoofs on the sod, but he didn't hear any such sounds. Once he dozed off to sleep, he didn't know for how long, but he woke up and sat on the edge of his bunk and looked out of the small window toward the stable. It was bright moonlight out there. Sam hoped that any second he might see Mustang prancing around there, but there was no sign of him.

Sam pulled on his boots and quietly slipped out. He had tied Old Bill in the stable, and he thought that if Mustang came in he would stay with Old Bill as usual. Sam stood in the doorway of the stable and looked inside. He called softly, "Mustang, are you in there?" Sam heard the low friendly sounds from Old Bill, but that was all. He went up to Old Bill and patted him a little and said, "I expect that if you could talk you would tell me why Mustang don't come in. Well, if he don't come in by daylight you and I will start out bright and early and we'll hunt him. But like as not we'll find him and maybe when he sees us he'll come running to meet us. He's still young—maybe he's forgot—just this one time." But Sam was very uneasy. Anyway, morning would soon come. Sam walked back to the house and in the stillness he went to bed.

III

A MEXICAN cowboy, known by the name of Mack, had drifted up from Old Mexico and this summer he had come into the region of the Horseshoe Ranch. However, none of the men at the Horseshoe had seen Mack; in fact, no one in this territory had seen him except the riders at the Almazan Ranch farther to the west. All that they knew about Mack was that he had stayed at the ranch for a week, that he was a good shot with a rifle, which he always carried in a holster on his saddle, and he was also a remarkably clever man with a rope. It happened that Mack owned nothing but his horse, the one he rode, which seemed to be the worse for hard riding. The men did not know that all that Mack wanted at this time was to get a good horse so that he could ride to the southern border and cross over into Old Mexico.

One day well along in the afternoon Mack was riding alone, a long distance from the Almazan Ranch, when he saw a horse that caused him to ride quickly into some woods and hide. He saw two horses, in fact, two that were standing close together and dozing in the warm sunshine. These horses were Mustang and Old Bill. They had wandered farther from the Horseshoe Ranch than ever before. But, if left alone, both would have returned as usual. It was Mustang that Mack wanted. He saw at once that Mustang was a young horse and a strong one—a tall, rangy horse, the kind that could run.

There was no wind that day to tell Old Bill and Mustang of the presence of the man hiding in the woods. And there was nothing to tell them that a man was there with a rifle and that he was a remarkably good shot. It must be admitted that Mack was different from most Mexicans of that day in that he *was* a good shot. He had more than once successfully "creased" horses and so captured them. To "crease" a horse meant to shoot at him so that the rifle bullet would strike him near the spine at the top of the neck. This would knock him unconscious and he would lie stunned, but only for a brief time, and when that brief time passed he would jump up and be as good as ever.

Mack was within easy rifle shot from where he hid. He dismounted from his old horse who was already standing with his head down, tired out and half asleep. Mack took a rest with his rifle on a dead limb near the trunk of a tree. The rifle cracked. Mustang fell and Old Bill, terrified, ran away. Mack mounted his old horse and spurred quickly to Mustang. One look and he saw that the bullet had only grazed Mustang's neck. But Mack must work swiftly. This he did with skill.

When Mustang came to himself he tried to leap to his feet and got half up, then he fell back. There were ropes on both his front legs so that they were held rather close together. But the next instant he tried again and this time he stood up, but when he tried to plunge he fell to the ground again. He lay for a second looking with wild eyes at Mack, and again Mustang got to his feet. He didn't try to leap this time. He didn't want to fall again. He only stood, trembling and waiting, trying like a wild horse to think how best to act here.

The cunning Mack was prepared for this. He put a hackamore, or rope halter, on Mustang's head with a long rope attached. Holding this long rope Mack picked up the saddle he had taken from his own horse and dropped it on Mustang's back. Mustang flinched. But the saddle did not frighten him so much. Sam had often put a saddle on him. It was the man here that was frightening. While Mustang stood trembling, with his forefeet tied, Mack reached under him, got the big broad girth and quickly cinched the saddle on Mustang.

Everything had happened so quickly to Mustang that he stood trembling and scared and still a little weak from the shock of it all. He stood while Mack slowly took the rope from his feet, then just as Mack grabbed the saddle horn and started to mount, Mustang began to fight. He whirled, but the skillful Mack swung up into the saddle as easily as a bird might fly to a nest.

When Mustang saw that the man on his back stayed on, he decided to get him off. With a snort he leaped quickly to one side and out on the plain and bucked with all his power. So high did he leap and whirl and plunge that Mack, top rider though he was, time after time was nearly thrown, but he stayed in the saddle. And after a while Mustang stopped bucking and stood still, his feet wide apart, his nostrils distended while he puffed with exertion. His once bright bay

coat was dark with sweat. Now Mack tapped
him with the end of the halter rope. Mustang
sprang forward and, not knowing what else
to do, he galloped away rapidly, and Mack
was pleased since this was what he wanted
Mustang to do. He wanted him to go toward
the south and he wanted him to go as fast
and as long as he could. Fortunately for Mustang the day was far spent when he was captured and as he galloped on and the darkness
fell, the cool of the night revived him.

Mustang all at once slowed down to a
walk. The Mexican, who had lost one of his
spurs, began to gouge Mustang with the
other. Suddenly Mustang reared up so high
and quickly that he lost his balance and fell
over backward. Only Mack's skill saved his
own life. He got out of the saddle and when
Mustang, considerably jarred from the fall,
got to his feet, Mack leaped back in the saddle. He decided, however, that here was a
horse that would not stand punishment from
a spur. Mack mumbled to himself, "He's a

crazy horse. He's big, swift, but he's crazy.
I be careful and I trade him. I trade him off
for another horse on account he's crazy!"

Horses, and sometimes mules and oxen,
were the main source of transportation in
these days, and horses especially, if they were
even fairly good ones, could always be sold
or traded to advantage.

Mustang, at a gentle tap of Mack's hand,
started forward, but he only walked. And
now Mack began to use his cunning brain.
He knew where there was a wagon trail—a
trail where men in "prairie schooners," or
covered wagons, were crossing the plains, and
it came to him that if he could keep Mustang
going until morning he might possibly trade
him to one of these travelers for another
horse.

Presently they came to a small stream in
the low plain and here Mustang was allowed
to stop and drink. After he had drunk of the
cool water he felt refreshed and he walked
across the shallow sandy place to the other

side, and when his captor tapped him slightly with the end of the halter rope he set out in an easy canter, and to Mack's surprise, Mustang held this pace for a long time. He seemed now not to tire and Mack had half a mind to keep him. But well along in the night two things happened that made the Mexican change his mind quickly. The first was that he came upon a wagon trail and the second was that, without thinking, he gouged Mustang with the spur. Instantly Mustang reared high and stood straight up. He did not fall over backward this time but he was so near to it that Mack was scared and disgusted. He knew now that he would trade him at the first chance.

He kept Mustang moving along the wagon trail in the starlight into the middle of the night when Mack decided to sleep. Arrived at a tree near the trail he tied Mustang and, moving off a little distance, Mack slept for a few hours. On awakening he mounted

Mustang and continued along the wagon trail.

The dawn was just coming when Mack saw a small campfire just ahead of him. He rode up to find a lone traveler—a short, stocky man with a bushy dark beard. He had already cooked and eaten his breakfast and was about to hitch up his horses. Mack spoke to the man, who introduced himself as Cole Hunter. It turned out that he had two old plugs of horses, little more than skin and bones, and also a tough, wiry broncho that was led behind the wagon. Cole Hunter and Mack talked for a time and a trade was made. Mack said that he would trade Mustang for the tough broncho because the broncho could stand travel and Mustang couldn't as he was too young. Cole was clever. He knew the broncho could not be made to pull the wagon. He had tried him. The animal would try to kick everything to pieces, then he would lie down. Mustang could, at least, be no worse. So the trade was made.

The saddle was put on the broncho. The Mexican mounted and, after the usual spell of bucking, the broncho galloped away at a fast pace. With a wave of his hand, Mack, who was the cause of all Mustang's trouble, rode away toward the border.

Cole Hunter did not intend to be cruel to his horses. He was simply, as he thought, practical. He let the poorest of his old horses loose, and, with Mustang tied to the wagon, he put the harness on him. Mustang was very tired and hungry after his long journey and could not fight as he would have done if he had been rested. Even so it took the man, who was skilled with horses, some time to get Mustang hitched up with the old horse, but this was finally done. While Cole did not want to be cruel he did want to get to his distant destination. It seemed to him that Mustang, being in good flesh, should pull most of the load and, accordingly, Cole put what was known as a stay-chain on the double-tree behind Mustang. In this way the old horse could, if the driver allowed him, lag back a little and Mustang would have to pull the whole load. This was a common practice in these days, to put a strong horse with a small one or with an old, weak horse. Fortunately this was a light wagon with only a small load in it.

When Cole was ready he got up in the seat of the wagon and shouted, "Giddap!" The old horse understood. He started forward. But to Mustang this was all new. Mustang stood still. But when he felt a whip touch him he jumped forward. He then tried to run away, but no matter how much he leaped and plunged he found all those straps and chains still stayed on him, and no matter how much he tried to pull the wagon faster it only seemed to get heavier and harder to pull. Mustang didn't know that when he tried to plunge and run he was then pulling the whole wagon by himself. He could not understand anything about all this. But after he fought in this way for some time he was so tired he became quiet and simply walked along beside the old, skinny horse. In fact, Mustang realized for the first time that the horse was beside him, and when he looked at the old bony horse walking slowly along, Mustang felt a little better. He tried to put his nose over to the horse to be friendly but the horse only opened his eyes a little and just went plodding along as if he were half asleep. This skinny horse was very old, almost twenty years of age. All his life he had pulled a wagon and nothing interested him any more except rest. He wanted only to eat grass and rest and sleep—nothing more. Mustang couldn't understand this. When he saw how the old horse acted, Mustang again stepped along, pulling the load, his head up, his eyes open wide, looking for something to happen so that he could get away from this thing. If he could have talked like the cowboys he would have called it "an awful mess," for that's what it was to him.

After a time Mustang was covered with

sweat and he wanted a drink of water. The old horse had been allowed to drink at a little stream near the camp, but Cole Hunter thought Mustang would tame down quicker if he got weak from lack of water. When he got Mustang well in hand he would let him have water and grass. If Cole had known all that Mustang had in him he would have taken better care of him so that some day he could have got a big price for him, but fortunately for Mustang, Cole did not know this. He merely looked on Mustang as just another horse who was young, maybe worth a little more than the average, but that was all.

The time dragged until late forenoon. Finally Cole stopped and let both horses drink at a small pond. Then he let them rest for two hours. The old horse was let loose to graze. Mustang was tied with a stout rope and allowed to eat grass. But before Cole unhitched him he tied a short rope on Mustang's front feet and in this way hobbled him.

Mustang could now graze at the end of the long rope tied around his neck and if he broke it he still would be hobbled so that he could be caught. But Mustang did not try to get away. He ate grass as fast as possible and when Cole at last hitched him to the wagon Mustang felt much refreshed. He tried to jump about and get free but his two front feet were tied so closely together that Cole managed him and he was again hitched up to the wagon beside the old horse. Cole then took the hobble from his feet and again at the word "Giddap!" the old horse started forward. Mustang lunged back once but felt the whip, then he lunged forward and again he stepped along, pulling nearly all of the load because of the stay-chain fixed to the doubletree behind him.

As Mustang plodded along through the long afternoon he became very tired and Cole Hunter began to see that he was not likely to reach the western town he was heading for unless he could meet another traveler and trade the old horse for one who at least had strength to pull a little and so help Mustang.

Mustang walked slowly along the wagon trail on the level prairie, looking ahead for some sign that might tell him he would get out of this situation. But mile after mile it seemed the same. As he plodded along he was startled a little when a great flock of prairie chickens flew up ahead of him, and for a moment their light-colored breasts shone like a great bright flower against the blue of the sky. Mustang saw the birds fly away in their freedom. Two antelopes with their short tails stood off, well out of rifle range, and looked at Mustang pulling the wagon. Then they, too, in their joy of freedom raced away like a streak across the plain.

Presently the trail led near a narrow, shallow stream with green fringes of willows on either side. The afternoon sun shone very warm as Mustang pulled the wagon behind him. He was thirsty, and he wanted a drink so much that he licked his lips time after time. But Cole sat on the wagon seat smoking his pipe and paid no attention to Mustang except to see that he kept moving. At one point the trail turned out in a wide detour away from the stream, and still the wagon rolled along on the level plain.

Mustang saw ahead of him on the trail a crow walking about contentedly while its black wings glistened in the sunlight. At the near approach of the wagon the crow flew away and alighted on a small tree where it looked at the slow-moving wagon going by.

Farther on the wagon trail led between a range of steep hills and a shallow stream. Mustang, toiling along the road, was suddenly aroused when, close to the trail, he saw something on a big flat rock. Mustang stopped, snorted and looked at the hideous thing on the rock. Cole looked and he saw it also. It was an enormous rattlesnake. The rattler lay on the flat rock with its head raised up from its coils. The old horse who was on the side nearest the rock could have been bitten if he had not been stopped. He had only strength enough to snort a little and look at the big snake. Cole took a rifle from behind the seat and, taking careful aim, he shot the rattler through the head and so ended it. Mustang snorted and tried to run when he saw the flopping of the big rattler. The scare put a little life in him and he walked on with more energy for a time, but his new exertion did not last and he began again to lick his lips for want of water.

A mile farther and Mustang saw that the trail led down to the stream. This was a shallow ford in the small river where wagons crossed and here Mustang and the old horse were allowed to put their heads down and drink while they stood in the water that reached to their knees. It seemed to Mustang that he would never get enough water. He drank in great, quick draughts, filling himself as fast as he could, but Cole, watching him, presently pulled on the lines and compelled Mustang to lift his head. He took a long breath and did not feel as thirsty as when his head was down at the water. Experienced horsemen understood this. A horse that was famished for water on a hot day might easily drink too much and if he was made to lift his head up and look around for a time he would not drink so much. Cole shouted at both horses and they moved on across the stream. Mustang, now refreshed from the water, pulled doggedly on, but he felt a growing weariness because he needed food.

They had gone no great distance from the river when a covered wagon appeared, coming from the opposite direction. The wagon came slowly on and the teams met. This traveler, a tall, slim man, was driving a mule and a horse. Both the horse and the mule were in fairly good flesh but it was seen by Mustang's driver that the mule was old and gray about the face. Still a mule was a mule as long as he could walk, and it was plain to Cole that he might not be able to get to his distant town as matters stood. After some bickering, in which Cole paid a little cash, the old horse was traded and the mule was hitched beside Mustang. The small cash difference paid to get the old mule was what counted. After the trade was made Mustang's driver took off the stay-chain from the doubletree and now as the wagon moved along the mule took his share of the load.

Cole, sitting on the seat driving, smoked his pipe constantly, and sometimes a light breeze carried the scent of the smoke to Mustang's nostrils. The only effect it had on him was that it made him remember when the scent came to him that men were always nearby.

For a long time the only sounds to be heard were those of the wagon wheels as they rolled over a long stretch of ground covered with small pebbles and stones. The old mule plodded along as if he were half asleep but he pulled his share of the load. Mustang kept his eyes wide open, always watching. As he looked forward he saw in the distance,

near a dip in the plain, a number of large
birds flying slowly in circles above the place.
As he helped pull the wagon nearer he saw a
dark object in the low place beyond. Mustang
did not understand but his driver did. Cole
looked at the big birds flying above the place
and muttered aloud, "Some feller kept his
old horse too long and had to let him go to
the buzzards. I'm lucky I traded for this
mule. I'll be able now to get to the town and
I'll get a good trade for this young bay horse.
He'll strike the eye of the cowboys. Some
feller can feed him up and make a champion
bucker out of him maybe."

After a long time Cole Hunter saw the
western town ahead of him. Mustang saw it
too, and he was at once interested. What he
wanted was to have all these straps and chains
and, especially, the collar on his neck and
shoulders taken off. When quite near the
town the wagon reached a gentle slope. As
they came to the slope the wagon pushed up
against Mustang, but the old mule, with long

experience, leaned back in the broad breeching of his harness, while he took short, halting steps forward. At the same time Mustang felt the bridle bit in his mouth pulled hard by Cole who drew back on the lines. Cole also pulled back the iron lever that put the brakes on the iron tires of the hind wheels. This caused a screeching sound as the iron wheels rolled and jerked against the brake, and Mustang was frightened, but the old mule beside him paid no attention, just leaned back in his breeching. Mustang did the same although his breeching tickled him and he had a desire to kick, but the weight of the wagon pressed so hard against him that he could do nothing but step awkwardly along with the mule on the other side of him.

They came down the slope at last and to some level ground on the edge of the town. A little farther on was a big corral in which were horses and close beside this corral was a railroad track. But Mustang did not notice this. And even if he had he would not have

known what it was. He would not have
known that what were called "horse cars"
moved along on these tracks to carry horses
like him to the horse markets of the East,
where horses were sold to men who would
ride them or hitch them up to pull heavy
loads in wagons. All that Mustang knew was
that he saw many horses in the big corral
here, and also many men standing around the
corral. He was interested, too, in the many
horses he saw beyond the corrals and in the
sounds that came to him. But what interested
Mustang most were the mounted cowboys he
saw riding along the streets of this western
town. Two of the cowboys rode leisurely past
where he stood hitched to the wagon, but
they were busy in conversation and did not
notice him. When Mustang saw these men
in their wide-brimmed hats he pricked up his
ears with interest because they reminded him
of Sam McSwain. And now he saw other
cowboys riding here and there and he looked
intently at them. It seemed to him that Sam

might be with them. And if Sam had been
with those men who rode nearest, Mustang
no doubt would have recognized him and
nickered to him. For Mustang had not forgotten. It was merely that he did not know
where Sam was.

After Cole had looked ahead for a brief
time he drove Mustang and the mule up near
the big corral where the men were standing.
These men had just bought the horses in the
corral and they were talking about the matter of shipping them away. Cole stopped his
queer team and told the horse buyers he would
like to trade Mustang and the mule for another team of horses. The horse buyers gave
only a glance at the old mule hitched up with
Mustang. They knew the mule was of no
value to them, and they would not want him.
But they looked at Mustang with interest. In
these days, when shrewd men knew horses,
not many questions were asked in a horse
trade. All three horse buyers saw instantly
that Mustang was an unusually good horse

and after a little dickering they traded two "work" horses for Mustang, and traded even.

Mustang was now unhitched from the wagon. He was tired, hungry and thirsty, but he would break away if he could. The men worked carefully. They got a long rope on his neck and when the harness had been pulled off one of the men started to lead Mustang to the corral gate to put him in with the other horses. When Mustang saw that he was free, except for the man pulling on the rope, he leaped aside swiftly and almost broke the man's hold on the rope, but the other two men grabbed the rope, and although Mustang leaped and plunged to get away, these strong men dug their boot heels in the ground and held him. When Mustang saw that they could hold him he stopped and, looking at them, snorted. The three men held him and began talking among themselves.

"He's young and he's a fighter, ain't he!"

"You bet he is. He's half starved, but he's

a fighter. Looks like he's got race stock in him!"

"That's so, and he'll fetch a good price if we're careful and get him safe on the stock train."

Mustang stood his ground, his head up, his eyes wide, watching the three men. Slowly one of them took the dangling end of the long rope and tied it around a post at the gate of the corral. The man then opened the gate a little. Mustang couldn't get loose now unless he broke the rope. One of the men went into the corral and drove all the other horses back, for these horses in the corral had become curious at seeing Mustang and they were crowding close to the gate to look at him. When the horses inside had been driven back the gate was opened wide. Two men got well behind Mustang and one of them threw a rope and made it roll like a wave on the ground toward him. The end of the rope struck Mustang like a small whip. He leaped forward and into the corral, and the gate was quickly shut. With Mustang now inside and still tied to the post, the men approached him carefully. One of them said, "He's no ordinary stock. He's got fine blood in him. But he's a nervous horse, the kind that might fight us unless we're gentle with him."

At this moment a man with a load of hay drove up to the corral and, with a pitchfork, began tossing hay into the corral for the horses to eat. There were twenty or more horses in this corral, all colors and different sizes. They rushed for the hay, squealing, and some of them kicked the others when they reached it. Many of them laid back their ears, and with open mouths they drove back the others.

One of the men looked at Mustang, grinned, and said, "Let's untie the rope on his neck and let him loose with the others. I'll bet he gets his share of hay!" Very carefully this was done. At once Mustang started toward the hay. A few of the worst fighting horses were eating and holding the others back. Mustang walked rapidly up to them. A big sorrel horse laid back his ears and with gleaming teeth reached for Mustang. Mustang dodged, whirled and kicked that horse so hard he staggered. And then Mustang started in biting and kicking in such a way that it was no time until he had all the horses standing back. He stood looking at them for an instant, then snorted his contempt. They all understood. Presently Mustang grabbed up a mouthful of hay, then turned and faced them while he chewed rapidly on it.

These men of the West all grinned with admiration. One of them said, "He's saying to them horses, 'Going to starve me, are you? Huh! Why, if you do that again I'll chaw you up and spit you out in little pieces! I won't have it!'"

Mustang now began to eat ravenously of the hay. The other horses moved in a little below him and also began to eat, but while they chewed on their food they stood looking at Mustang. He was the kind they could not chase away. After a little Mustang saw the water in the trough at one end of the corral. Chewing a mouthful of hay, he started toward it. Two of the worst fighters were already there drinking. Mustang approached at a rapid walk, his ears laid back, and the two horses ran away. Mustang reached down and with his big upper lip flipped the top of the water back a few times and then began to drink.

IV

THE night came with the stars shining brightly. As Mustang stood in the corral and looked over the top boards toward the town he had a great desire to escape. The corral was built of strong boards which were nailed to the posts on the inside so that if the horses crowded against the corral the boards would not come off but would be pressed the tighter against the posts. Mustang was taller than any of the other horses, so that as he stood looking over the corral his head and all of his great neck were above the top board. Now that he had shown all of the other horses that they had better let him alone he began to walk around inside the place, stop-

ping now and then to look over the corral at
the forms of the men he saw moving about.
At times some of the men walked so near that
he heard the low jingling sounds made by
what was called "bells" on the spurs. Not all
spurs were equipped with these bells but all
spurs had round sharp wheels. Mustang did
not know that these sounds came from the
large wheel-spurs on the boots of the cowboys and he merely looked with suspicion at
the men themselves. He had never heard this
jingling sound when Sam McSwain was on
his back for Sam wore no spurs at all when
mounted on Mustang.

After several hours passed, all the other
horses accepted the situation. They had
stopped milling around and stood in small
groups, half asleep. But Mustang was wide
awake. He wanted to get out of here. In this
place everything seemed strange and unnatu-
ral. And back in his mind he wanted to get
to the *one* man he knew so well. Life was as
he wanted it with Sam.

Mustang wanted to be free. That was as far as he could think at this moment and he felt a new confidence that he might get free because there was no strap or rope on him. It seemed to him that if he could get out of this corral he could run away and remain free.

The time dragged on until about two o'clock in the morning. There were not so many sounds in the town now and Mustang could see some dim lights on only one street as he stood looking over the corral fence. He did not know that those lights were in the saloons, that they always burned all night and that men were in them, some of these men evil characters who laid their schemes while sitting in the dark corners of these taverns.

So it was that while Mustang looked down the street of this strange town, he did not know that he was being talked about by two men who sat at a table in a dimly lighted corner of one of the saloons. One of the men was tall and thin, known by the name of

"Slim." The other man was short and of stocky build, known as "Mose." The plan of Slim and Mose concerning Mustang was simple. They were familiar with a certain cattle town a long distance from this place. Many cattle were brought to this town by cowboys, for shipment to the East. The two men had decided to take Mustang out of the corral and, with a rope on his neck, travel with him to the distant cow town where there were so many cowboys. Mose and Slim believed Mustang could be made to buck, and buck hard. They would see about this and, if so, they would bet the cowboys that they could not ride him.

Slim and Mose spoke in undertones for some time, then they went out and looked toward the corral where Mustang and the other horses were. The men had their own horses tied outside to a post on the street.

As Mustang stood looking down the street he saw the two men, who had mounted their horses, approaching. He watched them until they came close to the corral, where they stopped. He did not know that they were talking about him. He heard only the low sounds that came from them. Mose said, "There he is, Slim! He's well separated from the others. Let's tie our horses here to the corral so they'll keep his attention. Then we can sneak in at the gate and one of us can get a loop over his head with our ropes."

These two men were experienced and skilled with horses. When Mustang saw the two horses tied to the corral so close to him and when he saw the men disappear, he put his nose over to the horses and, as they happened to be the friendly kind, his mind was all on them. He did not see two shadowy forms sneak in the gate at the other end of the corral. He was still looking at the two horses, and he made friendly sounds to them as they did to him. Some of the horses standing together on the other side of the corral only looked and did not move, for the men

were not coming in their direction. They
were sneaking toward Mustang.

Mustang was so occupied with the two
friendly horses that he did not see what
was happening until Slim moved out of the
shadow made by the corral fence. Mustang
snorted and turned. As he did so Mose, who
was nearby in the shadows, threw his rope.
The loop settled over Mustang's head and he
felt it quickly tighten. He stood still, trembling. Mustang was, as the cattlemen said,
"rope-broke." What was meant by this was
that when, for the first time, a young horse
was caught with a rope that was tied at the
other end to a post or a tree, and he tried to
run, he would be thrown hard. Sometimes a
young horse might even lose his life in falling. It was one of the hard ways in the West
to break and tame a horse. Sam McSwain had
not wanted Mustang to be rope broke in this
way, but one day when Mustang was nearly
three years old he had been tied to a long rope
fixed to a tree not far from the ranch. A

wolf ran out of a ravine and so close that Mustang was scared and ran as hard as he could. When he got to the end of the rope he was thrown so hard that he could "see stars." Sam saw this happen, and he hurried up to Mustang and made him easy, but Mustang never forgot. After that he was always rope-broke. If a rope was thrown over him he stood trembling, afraid almost to move. At times a rope-broke horse was tied to a long rope at night and, finding he was at the end of it, he would pull back steadily and try to break it. But he would not *run* against it.

Mose whispered, "It's O.K.! He's rope broke. Lead him out." The men did not trouble to fix the rope on Mustang's neck. It was in a slip knot and would choke him if he tried to run, but the men were certain he would do nothing now but follow. They believed the rope would tame him, and they were right in their belief.

The two men led him to the gate and they purposely opened the gate wide and left it open. They knew that all the other horses in the corral would escape, and with so many horse tracks going in so many directions, the tracks of their own horses and those of Mustang would not be distinguished from the others.

Mose and Slim mounted their horses and led Mustang away. They rode at a gallop over the plains in the night, one of them in the lead, with Mustang's rope on the saddle horn, and the other man coming on close in the rear to keep Mustang going at a steady pace.

Mustang wanted to leap aside and run away but this rope was to him a deadly thing. If he lagged back the rope would pinch his neck, so he kept close to the horse galloping in front. He found that when he kept close to the horse in front the rope hardly pinched at all, for there was a little slack in it. Mose and Slim were careful not to hurry him too much and they did what they could to prevent the rope on his neck from jerking suddenly. It was not their intention to hurt Mustang unless he tried to break away. Mose and Slim would not have classed themselves as bad men. They were unlearned, unusually crude men. To them, as to many others in these crude days of the Old West, physical force and stealth was one way of making a living. Their method here in no sense troubled them. The only thing that gave them and others of their kind any concern was that they might be caught.

The two riders traveled on at a steady gallop. Late afternoon of the first day they reached a low valley covered with green grass near a small watercourse. Here they stopped and, after letting the horses drink, they tied each of them well apart on their long ropes so they could eat grass. The men carried with them what was known as "jerked" beef, which was simply dried beef. This was their food and for the horses there was the grass along the way.

After night came the men lay down and

slept several hours. Then they again mounted their horses and rode away, leading and driving Mustang as before. Several days passed this way until, about noon one day, they came in sight of the western town which was their objective.

They rode their horses at a walk as they approached the town, and when they came to the edge of it, they stopped before a well-made stable with a high corral built out from one side. Mose, who was in the lead, dismounted, opened the gate, and led his horse and Mustang into the corral. There were no other horses here at this time.

Suddenly the door of the stable opened and two men came out into the corral. At once the two men looked at Mustang and then they looked knowingly at each other. It was plain that the two men who owned this place were not much surprised to see Mose and Slim. One of them said, "Well, Mose, you and Slim got a good horse this time. He's big enough and he's stout enough. Now, he looks like the kind we've been wanting for a long time. If he'll buck, and buck hard enough, we'll make money. There are plenty of cowboys who will bet they can ride him, but we got to know what he'll do first."

There was some more talk among the four men and the two horses that Slim and Mose had ridden were taken outside of the corral and tied to a post. Then a saddle was put on Mustang. He did nothing when they put the saddle on him, for they did not hurt him. He was used to this procedure; it was no different from the way Sam McSwain put the saddle on him. But he stood watching the men. Mustang already had had one new experience when a strange man, the Mexican, Mack, got on his back. He had for the first time felt the sting of a spur in his side. These men noted that while Mustang stood still as they cinched the saddle on him, he watched them like a hawk. The men had seen a few of the worst bucking horses do this. And already Mustang looked promising to them. He was so much taller and stronger than the average horse that they were sure they could make money on him by betting the cowboys who frequented the town that they could not stay on him. It was only a question of whether he would buck good and hard.

When Mustang stood saddled and ready one of the men who owned the stable said, "Well, Slim, you and Mose are both good riders. One of you try him. See what we got. There's no one around to watch us. One of you get on him."

Both Mose and Slim wore spurs as did the cowboys generally. In these days they all spurred their horses. They spurred them if they bucked, and even if they did not buck a rider would spur the horse simply to start him forward and he spurred him again if he wanted him to go faster. Spurs were the most common thing used in riding all western horses. And if a horse shied at anything and bucked they spurred him all the more because it was thought that this was the way to get a horse in hand—spur him hard and make him know this man was his master. The men supposed that if Mustang was a bucking horse he could be made to fight hard in this way.

Slim said he would mount Mustang. The corral was free of objects except a large manure pile close to the barn. And with this exception the ground was level. The men had carefully fixed the rope on Mustang's neck so that it could no longer slip. It was cut off so that the end of the rope was all the rider would hold in his hand. A rope halter or just a rope like this one around the horse's neck was all these men used in riding a bucking horse. They didn't care how much he bucked. He could have his head and do as he pleased. And as a rule, if it was an average bucking horse, a good rider could stay on. Some horses were blindfolded so that while one man held him the cowboy could come up, sneak one foot in the stirrup and even sneak up in the saddle. But it was known that with some of the worst bucking horses it was not necessary to blindfold the horse or sneak up on him. The horse might stand still while the cowboy put his foot in the stirrup and took hold of the saddle horn, and still stand until the rider swung into the saddle. But the instant that happened the horse started things.

These men all believed Mustang was that kind of horse. They did not know that if he was not touched with a spur he would not fight. While the men were about to try Mustang they did not know that he had no bucking tricks. They did not know that whatever Mustang did to defend himself he would have to do by instinct. It was true he had reared up and fallen over backward with the Mexican and he had reared up again later, but that was the only time he had done it. All he could do now was the first thing instinct prompted him to do. So it was that Mustang did not know what he would do here and he did not, as yet, know what the men were going to do. But he stood watching them and to him they already seemed men that he could not trust.

Slim took the end of the rope that was on Mustang's neck. The other men got well back. Slim slowly took hold of the saddle horn and slowly he put his left foot in the stirrup on the left side of Mustang. Then up he swung and as he came down on the saddle he acted by force of habit and gouged Mustang hard with both spurs. When Mustang had thrown the Mexican he had been so frightened that he hardly knew what he did, but now he felt both frightened and angry. He decided to get the man off his back in a hurry. The result was that he leaped high and bucked with such force that in no time he threw Slim high in the air, so high that Slim came down on his face on the big manure pile. There was loud laughter from the men. Slim got up, wiping the dirt and straw from his face, at the same time saying he would bet no man could stay on Mustang.

At this moment four other cowboys heard

the sounds and came up to the corral. They were all good riders and when they found that the big bay horse had just thrown his rider they said they would take a chance on riding him. A tall, bowlegged cowboy was selected by one of the men who owned the barn and the cowboy slowly approached Mustang. Mustang retreated to one side of the corral, but other men walked up so that the cowboy could get up close and mount. The tall, bowlegged cowboy took hold of the end of the rope that was tied to Mustang's neck. He slowly took hold of the saddle horn and put his foot in the stirrup, then swung quickly up in the saddle. The men ran in every direction, for Mustang started plunging and bucking, and this man, like the first, began to spur him on both sides.

Although Mustang was new at bucking he had already learned something. Now, knowing how he had bucked one cowboy off, Mustang knew what to do, and he began to be aware of his own power in this matter. He

leaped high, came down on the ground hard, kicked his hind legs high in the air, and when his hind feet struck the ground again he leaped up high and came down with his back bowed and his four legs stiffened. The powerful shock by this big horse threw the rider—threw him to one side where he hit the ground hard and rolled in the dust. He got up, his face covered with dirt, and he grinned while the dozen men, who had now come up, shouted and laughed at the procedure.

The two men who owned the stable talked in low tones to Mose and Slim. These owners began to see unusual opportunities for making money by getting still other riders to try to ride Mustang. They knew that the main pride of a cowboy was that he could ride even the worst horse.

On this first day many good riders among the cowboys put up their bets and mounted Mustang. Some of them were able to stay on his back longer than others, but he threw

them all. All of them spurred him in the sides and some of them used their quirts, or short whips, on him to tame him. These riders thought that since this method tamed other horses they would tame this horse even though he was big and powerful. But Mustang threw the last man as hard as he did the first one.

That night Mustang found oats in his feed box. A man came in later and filled two buckets with water for him. Mustang's sides, where the men had spurred him, stung and smarted so much that he switched his tail from sheer discomfort. He was tired from all his exertion but he was young and somehow he managed to get his rest this night although he slept fitfully.

It did not occur to these men that they were being cruel to Mustang. They actually admired him for his quickness and his power. To them he was an unusual horse in build and power but was still a horse to be ridden and mastered in the usual way if the rider was skillful enough.

It was past noon of the next day when the men again put the saddle on him and took him out in the corral. There were many men present to ride him on this afternoon and matters went on much as the day before. The first man who got on him was quickly thrown. And so were many others. But after the time had gone by and man after man had fought with him, Mustang, young and strong though he was, began to feel the strain and he had to buck and fight for some time to get the rider off. Finally, because of the spurs that gouged him, he became wild with rage. At last, when a man got on him, Mustang did an unusual thing, something very few horses did. When he had thrown this rider he whirled and, with ears laid back and long teeth gleaming, he rushed for the man. Mustang would have bit and trampled his tormentor but the man got out of his way by crawling under the lower boards of the corral.

Instead of wanting to punish Mustang for this, all the men thought it was his right to do as he pleased. In fact, they all saw in him a most unusual horse. It was decided that he could rest until the next day. The two men who owned the barn came up to him cautiously, took the saddle from his back, and got him into the box-stall in the stable where he was to remain for the night. Mustang was now wholly free in the stall, for they even took the rope off his neck.

When Mustang was aware that he was alone he walked around in the stall looking for an opening, but he found none. Later, he was startled somewhat at seeing a man stop in an alleyway in front of the stall. The man put a good feed of oats in the feed box for Mustang. Another man, as before, set two buckets of water in the stall. Then both men went away.

For some time Mustang stood and looked

about him in the gathering darkness. He was
not hungry, but he was thirsty. He went to
one of the buckets of water, smelled it a little
and drank some of it. But he drank only a
little. After looking and listening for some
time he again drank of the water and after
looking and listening again for some time, he
drank all that was in one bucket, and after
a little while he drank all the water in the
other bucket. Again he watched and listened.
Complete darkness had come now. He could
hear no sounds in the barn except in one of
the stalls, some distance away, where an old
horse had been tied and was eating the hay in
his manger. It happened that he was the only
other horse in the barn at this time. When
Mustang heard the other horse munching hay
he felt hungry and he went up to the feed
box where the man had put the oats. He
smelled the grain carefully as a sensitive horse
always does when confined in a strange place.
To Mustang here, not only the barn and the
men but even the water in the buckets and

the oats set before him were strange, and he looked at everything with suspicion.

After he had eaten the oats and drunk the water Mustang stood and listened for sounds, but he could hear nothing about the place except the lone horse at one end of the barn as the animal moved about in his stall. After a long time the other horse became still, for he was standing and dozing in the night. Mustang peered into the darkness across his manger but he could see nothing.

The time dragged but Mustang remained as wide awake as ever. There was a swelling now on each of his sides where the spurs of the men had cut him, and the wounds annoyed him. All at once he gave a start and looked toward the darkness across the manger. He heard a sound on the board floor of the alleyway in front of his manger. It was a soft sound, several of them in fact, and they were coming toward him. He was startled when a match was struck and its light flared up for a time. Mustang saw something he was not accustomed to—a human with a *dress* on, lighting the lantern.

This person was Mary Manning, a young woman whose home was nearby. On this day Mary had seen Mustang and the men in the corral from the front porch of her home. Mary, herself, rode horses and she knew and loved them. She knew that a high-spirited horse was sensitive and that he could always be handled easily if he was shown kindness by those who had the care of him. Mary had seen so much of this punishment of horses here of late that she determined to do all she could to stop it. She knew from what she had seen that Mustang was not only an unusual horse but he was a sensitive and beautiful one, and Mary had a clear conscience in what she was going to attempt here. She was going to give Mustang his liberty. She believed that quite possibly Mustang had been stolen. In any case, she planned that if she could leave the barn door open and turn him loose on the plains, the men would suppose a horse thief had stolen Mustang.

Mary reached across the manger and hung the lighted lantern on a nail on the side of Mustang's stall. From a pocket in her calico apron she took a red apple, and holding it toward Mustang, she said softly, "Come on up, Beauty. I don't know your name but I'm going to help you to get away. Come on up! They shan't punish you again if you'll trust me!"

There was something about the young woman's voice and manner that appealed to Mustang. She was holding the apple out. It smelled good and her low words reassured him. He stood for a little looking at her in the dim light of the lantern, then he moved near and put his nose out. She held the apple on her palm. Mustang touched it with his nose, then took it in his teeth and stood munching it while he looked at her. The girl then decided to go ahead with her plan. She went out and around and gently opened the door of Mustang's stall. He turned and saw her, and again he heard her low, quiet voice. He did not fear her in the least as she came up to him. He put his nose to her and she rubbed his head and patted him a little on his big neck. Then she reached up, took hold of his foretop and said, "I'll bet you lead well! Come on—let me lead you out!" She started out and Mustang followed. From the time Mustang was a year old Sam had taught him to lead by his foretop. When they reached the corral gate, Mary opened it, and taking his foretop again, she led him a quarter of a mile out on the open plain. Here she stopped and took another apple from her apron pocket. While Mustang ate it she patted him on the neck and said, "Now, Beauty, you are free! They can't cut you with their sharp spurs tomorrow—and never again if you'll always watch and run when you see them!"

Mustang finished the apple and stood

looking out on the starlit plain. Mary was afraid he might be seen. She stepped back and said, "Run now, run!" She clapped her hands, stamped her foot on the ground, and said, "Run away before they see you!"

Mustang did not know what she said but there was something in her manner that made him feel he was free to go. He started away at a walk, then he lifted his head and all at once he broke into a gallop. The farther Mustang galloped the more he wanted to run faster and so leave the town and all its men as far behind as possible. He traveled on through the night for miles before he stopped to refresh himself. Arrived at a low, green valley, he stopped long enough to graze a short time, then he again trotted away toward the west.

It was the afternoon of the next day when he walked up to a ridge and saw, just below him, three men on horses coming in his direction. Mustang stood looking at the riders and all at once they saw him. With a snort of defiance Mustang leaped to one side and went thundering past the riders only a short distance away. The three men looked and one among them gazed in pleased astonishment. It happened this man was Bud Allen from the far distant Horseshoe Ranch. Bud had been sent into this region on cattle business. He exclaimed, "Well, I be daggoned! It's Mustang! The white spot on his chest, his white legs! Him big as life and as purty!" As the men watched Mustang, he ran like a deer across the plain toward the west, and on and on he ran. Bud said, "Well, all I can do now is to tell Sam. When I get back I'll tell him I saw Mustang in this region. Maybe he stays up here and maybe he's headed back toward his home country. Anyhow, he's headed in the right direction. My guess is that if Sam ever gets track of him he'll get him. But he can't *run* him down."

The three riders sat on their horses and

looked at the great bay horse rapidly disap-
pearing in the distance. One of the men said,
"Bud, not even two dozen fellers on good
horses could ever catch that big bay. He's
too fast!"

V

WINTER had come to this place of
sheltered woods known as River Bend. Years
before, some men had built a crude stable of
logs and a cabin here and tried to farm the
ground on the plain nearby. But like many
others in these days, after a time they had
left this wild, forbidding country and gone
East where there were more people and
things which made life easier. But the
grizzled trapper, Vic Winters, who had come
upon this place, found it was just what he
wanted. There were beavers along the river
and Vic was trapping them. He could not
use the stable but he was now using the cabin
for his home. He had all the supplies he

needed for the winter, and he knew that in the springtime he could sell his furs and then spend the summer at his favorite ranch which happened to be the distant Horseshoe. Vic liked the men there and, in particular, he liked Sam McSwain, Jim Parkman and Bud Allen.

When Vic had taken possession of this place he noticed the stable in the timber by the river and he noted casually an old stack of hay there that the farmers had left, but to Vic such a thing as a stack of hay held little interest. However, his keen eyes saw that the hay was unusually well stacked and it was well covered with long slough grass. Vic knew that a stack of hay put up like this would keep for several years. His keen eyes had also noted that there was but one door in the stable and this faced the log cabin. But he paid no further attention to the stable as he passed each morning to run his trap line.

One morning while Vic was looking at his traps along the river he saw timber wolf tracks in the snow that had fallen early in the night. He thought little of this since he knew that gray wolves were in the vicinity. And he might have given them no further thought if he had not, farther on, come upon tracks other than those of gray wolves. Vic had just crossed a ditch in the woods near the river when he saw gray wolf tracks and also the tracks of a *horse*. Instantly Vic was all attention. He saw that only one horse had been traveling here and that there were three timber wolves, one of the wolves bigger than the others. Vic followed the trail. A little farther on the tracks led out of the woods and on across a level snowy waste, and he noted that the wolf trails still followed the horse. He saw that the horse and the three wolves had been running.

A half mile farther on Vic saw, by the tracks, that the horse had come to a stand and the tracks of the horse and the wolves told Vic that there had been a fight here. The wolves had attacked the horse but Vic read in the tracks that the battle had been brief and the horse had run on again. Vic, now keenly alert, followed the trail until it passed over a rise of ground where he saw, a little ahead of him, a big grayish form lying on the snow. Vic came up and his eyes opened wide. One of the gray wolves lay lifeless on the snow while the confusion of horse and wolf tracks here told of a fierce battle. There were spots of blood on the snow near the place where the timber wolf lay. Vic exclaimed, "Whew! Them wolves tackled that horse to bring him down but he was a fighter. He got one of 'em but the other two daggoned brutes still was after him. Hope they didn't hurt him much. But he ain't got much chance out here by himself. It's queer, him being all alone out here by himself. Wonder why there ain't some more horses with him. I can't figger out how he happens to be all alone. Never saw any range horses around here. He must have been lost from a traveler. Whew!" Vic exclaimed again, "he's a fighter and he's a big horse, too! His tracks show that and he must be mighty quick on his feet."

Vic followed the trail, noting that the horse had been running in long leaps while the two remaining wolves had run along on each side of the trail. He noted a few spots of blood on the snow on the horse's trail and he was sure this came from the horse. The old trapper guessed what had happened. The gray wolves must have charged the horse from the rear, trying to slash the hind tendon of the leg. This was their cunning manner of bringing down a horse on the range. If they succeeded in cutting the tendon the horse could not even walk, but Vic saw that the wolves had failed in that here. Evidently they had cut the flesh of the horse a little but that was all.

Vic, with his rifle on his arm and always ready, walked along the trail of the horse and the wolves for some time. His keen gray eyes saw not only the animal tracks near him but also the snowy wastes that lay ahead. And

at the same time Vic listened for sounds that
might come from the place beyond. Vic had
a double purpose in following the trail of the
horse and the gray wolves. First, like all men
of the Old West, he liked horses and it was
his desire to destroy the two wolves that were
following the horse and so save him. But as
Vic followed the trail he had another purpose in destroying the wolves. This was because they had been disturbing some of his
traps lately. He had seen wolf tracks about
the place along both the creek and the river
here.

So far as Vic himself was concerned he
had no fear of the wolves. He had his rifle
and he knew they would never attack him
unless he were down and helpless. Like other
trappers of these days, as Vic followed the
trail, he was clothed in a buckskin suit and a
fur cap on his head. The white landscape lay
very still on this winter day and for some
time Vic saw no sign of life. Then out from
the creek woods well forward he saw a big

gray owl fly low over the snow. The owl, on seeing Vic, turned and, still flying low over the snow, passed from sight in the woods beyond. "He's hungry," Vic muttered to himself. "He didn't get game last night. He don't like to hunt in the daylight but he's still hungry." A little farther on Vic said aloud, "That poor horse is hungry, too. No grass for him unless he paws down through the snow to it. He's had to do that, too, but I bet he's awful hungry. Now if he'll only find that old haystack at the stable he'll live. That is if he ain't too much scared of me and goes away when he sees my cabin close by, and also if the two daggoned wolves that's following him don't get him."

Vic followed the trail on for a time where it led around the foot of a hill. He walked to the turn in the hill, then suddenly he crouched behind a big boulder. Beyond him he saw where a hill fell away in a steep bank some fifty feet high. And there, with the steep bank to guard his rear, Vic saw the

horse fighting the two wolves! This was surprising enough, but Vic was even more surprised when he recognized the horse. Instantly he said, under his breath, "Why, daggone my hide, that's Mustang!" Vic might
not have been so certain, but on the instant he
crouched down to peer around the boulder
the horse was facing in this direction and Vic
saw not only the four white stocking legs but
the queer white spot on the horse's chest.
This mark was so distinctive, coupled with
the four white stocking legs, the black mane
and tail and the great size of the horse, that
Vic was sure he was looking at Mustang.
And he was amazed to see him so far away
from the Horseshoe Ranch in the dead of
winter. But there was *Mustang*, regardless of
how he had gotten so far away from the
Horseshoe and Sam McSwain.

The first thing Vic thought of now was to
get a chance to bring down at least one of the
gray wolves, but the situation was such that
the chances to do this were difficult. More-

over, when he fired, even if he had the luck
to bring down one of the wolves, the shot
would frighten Mustang so that he would
run away and so Vic might never see him
again. And he did not want that to happen
now.

While Vic fingered the trigger of his rifle
he knew that the wolves might take Mustang's life and that even though he scared
Mustang away, he must shoot at the first
wolf that got out a little way so there would
be no danger of striking Mustang. He saw
that neither wolf was taking too many chances
before Mustang's powerful front hoofs. One
of them rushed in as if to strike directly at
Mustang's front legs, then it swerved aside
and leaped for his hind leg, but Mustang
kicked so swiftly he nearly caught the wolf.
The other wolf now rushed up in front and
again Mustang stood with his tail to the high
bank. Vic heard Mustang snort. He saw him
stamp the snow in defiance and he heard him
snort again in his anger.

All at once a breeze sprang up and the wolves got the man scent. They rushed like two streaks across the snow and vanished in the woods. Mustang stood looking in wonder at them as they vanished. As Vic watched from behind the boulder he heard another of Mustang's loud snorts of angry defiance and again he saw him stamp the ground where he stood. Then Mustang walked out from the hill and, after taking another look in the direction the wolves had gone, he started back on his trail that led toward the river. Vic saw that he might pass near the rock and the trapper slipped around so that he could not be seen. On Mustang came. Plainly he had not scented Vic for when not more than a dozen yards from the rock he stopped, looked back toward the hill and snorted again.

The thought flashed through Vic's mind that if he could get near to Mustang and call his name he might get him to follow to the haystack at the stable and so pass the winter

there safely. Vic decided to take a chance.
He had never made as much fuss over Mustang as Sam and some of the other cowmen
had, but he had many times stood near him
and talked to him while Sam was brushing
him and had called his name. As Vic used to
say to Sam, he had only a "speaking ac-
quaintance" with Mustang. But Mustang
was, at least, acquainted with him. As he
stood looking back Vic called out twice,
"Mustang! Mustang!" Mustang started vio-
lently. He leaped back, and with his long
neck outstretched, his head low, his ears
cocked forward, he looked at Vic who was
now standing with his head and shoulders
above the boulder. At the same instant Vic
called again, "Mustang! Come, Boy!" That
was what Sam used to say to him. Vic knew.
Mustang leaped away and started to run but
he checked himself abruptly and stood looking at Vic who now stood out in plain sight
calling him by name. Mustang snorted,
looked at him again, then started off at a slow

trot, but he stopped once again and looked intently at Vic and again Vic called his name and used the same expression that Sam did, "Mustang! Come, Boy!"

Mustang blew through his nostrils and stood for a time looking at Vic. The snow covered all four feet of Mustang, but his white stocking legs and the rest of him showed against the white snow on the ground. His once bright bay coat of the summer was now a dull red with long hair standing unruly over his body, and his ribs showed plainly. That Mustang was nearly starving, Vic was certain when he looked at his wretched condition. Vic kept talking to him and calling him by name. "Mustang! Come, Boy! How did you ever come away out here? I bet you wish you was with Sam! I bet he wonders where you are. You're lost, that's what's the matter. Now, I'm going to cut across here and travel straight to my shack and if you'll follow me there's an old stack of hay there at the stable!"

Vic started off walking across the snow, going in a half circle well above the place where Mustang stood. Mustang blew through his nose again and started off as if he were going back over his trail, but Vic saw that when he himself entered the scattering woods some distance away, beyond which stood his shack and the stable, Mustang stopped and stood looking at him. Vic walked on through the woods and as he did so he looked back over his shoulder. To his great satisfaction he saw that Mustang started in this direction and he came on walking, though he seemed to be a little suspicious.

As Vic walked steadily on he managed to see all that Mustang did behind him. Mustang would follow for a little time, then stop, look inquiringly toward Vic, and he would look on either side where there was nothing but the cold snow and the silent, leafless trees. Vic walked slowly on but he did not stop, and three times he called out to

Mustang who kept well in the rear, "Mustang! Come, Boy! Come on with me! I'll get you some hay. Come, Mustang!"

Although Mustang was afraid here, afraid of things in general, these words of Vic were compelling. He did not understand all the words but he did know his own name and he knew Vic was calling him by his name. Not since he had been taken away from Sam and his home had he ever been called by his name until now. He was afraid of Vic as he had now become afraid of most men—all except Sam and his friends at the only home Mustang had ever known. But while he was afraid of Vic it was not quite the kind of fear he had of other men. Vic had called him by name and Mustang was cold and half starved. For weeks he had been cold, hungry and miserable. He did not know what would come of his following Vic through this cold, barren woods, and at times Mustang stopped and put his nose down to Vic's tracks in the snow and smelled them as if he wanted to trust a friend here but was still afraid.

Vic saw that if Mustang kept on in the direction he was going he would surely come near the old haystack at the stable. Vic, therefore, walked steadily on, at last coming to his cabin from which he could see the stable and the haystack. He at once went inside the cabin and peeped out of a small opening toward the stable.

Some time passed and there was no sign that Mustang was coming near, but finally Vic saw a movement in the woods beyond the stable and then he saw Mustang standing under the trees, his head up, looking toward the place where Vic lived. After a little time he saw Mustang start toward the stable. He walked slowly and he seemed to want to get to the haystack without being seen. As Vic watched he saw Mustang disappear behind the stable, then, a little later, he walked out into view and came near the hay. He stood for a little looking at the cabin, then, as if he thought it safe, he began to pull big mouthfuls of hay from the stack and eat. But while he did this he turned often to look at the house. Vic kept watching from the small opening, and he saw that Mustang was laying hold of the outside part of the stack and eating the old hay that had almost no nourishment in it. Mustang was so starved and afraid that he did not take time to pull out the outer part until he could reach the bright nourishing hay farther in the stack. Vic decided to help him.

He walked out of the cabin and called, "Mustang! Come, Boy! I'll get you some *good* hay!" Mustang walked off a little way and stood watching. Vic went to the stack and pulled out a lot of the good bright hay from deeper in the stack. He walked some distance away from this pile of good hay and told Mustang to come up and eat. Mustang did so, but as he ate ravenously he kept watching.

Vic was near enough to see the cuts on

Mustang's hind legs—cuts, he was sure, made by the gray wolves when they leaped for Mustang's legs to cut the tendons and bring him down. Vic mumbled to himself, "Daggone them wolves! They come purty close to getting him. But he showed 'em he's a fighter. He plumb discouraged one of 'em. Now *ain't* he a fine horse! And him about starved. And Sam don't know he's lost away off here. If he'll stay with me till spring I'll get him back to Sam."

Several times that day Vic pulled out good hay from the stack and left a pile of it for Mustang to eat. When he pulled out the last pile, toward evening, Mustang stood up very close, so close Vic could have touched him. But he didn't try to touch him, much as he wanted to rub him a little. He only called him by name and talked low and friendly to him. When Vic looked at Mustang's eyes he saw suffering in them, but he saw also, in spite of this, something not in the average horse. And those eyes told Vic that Mustang was half starved but there was the fire of fight in those eyes, too. This was something that an experienced man knew by just looking. Vic knew that Mustang had something in him that would make him fight as long as he could stand and he was the kind that would live when other horses would give up.

When it began to be dark Vic went in his cabin leaving Mustang eating the hay. Vic said to himself, "He'll stay and him and me is friendly and he knows it. And I got to help him if them daggone wolves tries to tackle him again. Maybe they'll be careful if they get my scent in the shack here. Still these daggone brutes are awful tricky when the dark comes." Vic went on talking to himself as was his custom. He said, "If Sam McSwain knew Mustang was way off here half starved, why, Sam would try to get to him, winter or no winter. Sam's awful set on that horse. Of course he don't look like much of a horse now—him with that awful long hair on him and his ribs all showing,

but if I can take care of him here until spring
I might be able to be so well acquainted with
him he'd let me set up on his back and ride
him to Sam. I'll see that he gets plenty of
nice bright hay from deep in the stack each
day." And with these words Vic at last ate
his supper and went to sleep on his bunk, but
he slept lightly. He awakened several times
that night and looked out. The night was
bitter cold with the moon shining and the
sullen winter wind blowing.

Vic awakened suddenly and he was no
sooner awake than he got his clothes on as
quickly as he ever had in his life. He heard
sounds out at the stable that told him the
wolves were attacking Mustang. A loud
strange sound that could come only from a
horse reached Vic's ears and he knew Mustang was in deadly peril, fighter though he
was. Vic grabbed his rifle and ran out in the
bitter wind. He saw Mustang was fighting
for his life, whirling and kicking and striking with his front hoofs, while the two big

wolves dodged and ducked low, driving in
for a slash at his hind tendons to bring him
down.

So furious was the battle and so strong the
wind in Vic's favor as he dodged among the
trees that he was almost on the scene before
the wolves were aware. He shot one of the
beasts and as the other darted away he fired
his repeating rifle quickly three times at the
wolf and it fell dead. Vic, with dire venge-
ance, fired two more shots into each of the
wolves to make certain they would, as he
said, "stay down permanent."

This done, he walked up slowly to Mustang who stood snorting and trembling. Vic
talked to him and after a little, strangely
enough, he got up to Mustang and began to
rub him and kept on talking to him. "Now,
Mustang, it's too daggone bad these two var-
mints tried to get you. I'm all worked up
myself knowing one slash from them in
the right place would have ruined you, but I
got 'em both and I reckon they're the same

two that was after you before. Don't be too much scared now. 'Tain't likely any others are around to tackle you. Anyway, I'm always close by."

Vic carried some hay into the stable and persuaded Mustang to come back in the shelter. After a time Vic went into his cabin but he stayed up and kept his eyes on the stable.

The weeks went by, and Mustang was living comfortably and safely at the stable. Every day Mustang would let Vic rub him and scratch his neck. One morning, a little after daylight, Vic heard a loud piercing nicker down by the river. He went to the place and saw Mustang. He seemed restless. He let Vic come up to him and scratch his neck and pat his big shoulder but he kept looking off in the distance toward the south. Vic said to him, "Mustang, I think you know that the grass is green in that direction maybe and you're hankering to go. And I'll bet you think of Sam now and then. But I hope you won't go off alone. I've got no rope to tie you and I know you want grass. Anyway, you have to be free to eat grass. It's so short here you have to be loose to get enough. But if you'll wait for a while some traveler will come along in a wagon and I'll take you to Sam and your old home. But of course I'm a feller and you're a horse and I guess you can't understand what I'm saying."

At last a morning dawned when Vic, to his great disappointment, could not see Mustang anywhere. The old man went down to the river but Mustang was not there. Vic followed his trail for an hour and he found that Mustang was traveling steadily toward the south. Vic still had hopes that he might see him, but the next day it was the same as before, and when a week more had passed Vic gave up. He said aloud, "He's traveling to the south where I think he somehow knows the grass is greener, but I don't think that's all of it. I think he wants to get home to Sam and the only thing he can think of is to travel. He knows Sam's not here and he don't know *where* he is, but it's natural for him to keep traveling. I hope he won't let any feller get a hold of him and my guess is he won't. He got to kinda liking me here because he was nearly starved and I took him in. He's likely been stolen from Sam and had hard treatment. But he's free now and he's likely to stay free. In time I'll see Sam and tell him. By traveling southward, Mustang can live on the green grass now, and if he keeps on in the direction he's going he'll be heading for the southwest and toward the Horseshoe Ranch. It may be possible Sam will see him before I do. Anyway, I'll see Sam in due time."

VI

RANGE horses of the Old West, if left alone, seldom wandered farther than fifty or sixty miles in any direction. These horses even made a home for themselves in the wild range country. But if a high-strung horse was forcibly taken far away from his home range and also given hard treatment by men, if he gained his freedom he was likely to become a wanderer with no fixed place whatever. Mustang had become such a horse. His strange experiences had taken him far from home and there was nothing upon which he could look that was familiar. Every valley and every stream, even every horse that he saw, all were strange and somehow all seemed forbidding. There was green grass to sustain life now, but in the heart of this gallant horse there was always a deep loneliness. Even though he grazed on the rich grass of some low, green valley by a quiet, woodland stream, this loneliness was in him. And it was in him when his physical hunger was satisfied and he stood in the starry night, half dozing, half sleeping, on a wild, western plain.

Mustang traveled slowly toward the southwest after leaving Vic. He took much time to eat of the green grass that was now growing everywhere. He was so hungry it seemed he couldn't get enough of it. And as the time went by he shed the long hair of his winter coat and his beautiful, bright bay color began to shine in the sunlight while his white stocking legs seemed all the whiter when he stood in some rich green valley biting off great mouthfuls of grass with his long and powerful teeth. He was now so far from his home that he had no notion of where it was. Even the wild horses, still farther to the southwest, had their grazing ground within certain limits, but it was not so with Mustang. He was a wanderer with all the strange restlessness that was constantly in a horse who no longer had his old home.

Mustang traveled many miles this spring, now and then seeing other horses, but for the most part, at such times he also saw men mounted on the horses and he kept on the move since he now dreaded men on horses above all others. He was still wandering aimlessly when autumn came. Then, one night in September, he came suddenly upon a scene that strangely interested him. As he walked over a ridge he saw, a little beyond him on a wide valley, the twinkling lights of a town, and at the same time many strange sounds came to his ears. Because it was night Mustang was not much afraid of the place with its many twinkling lights, although, because of his former experience, he associated the place with men. What interested him most was a few horses that he could see a little distance below as they stood grazing in the starlight.

Mustang walked out on the level plain and he moved slowly up to the horses. There were four of them. They were two teams of heavily built animals, known in these days simply as "work horses," and their work was that of pulling wagons with heavy loads in the town. These horses, being gentle and tame, were permitted by the men who owned them to graze on the outskirts of the town. The four horses paid no attention to Mustang when he came up but went on eating the green grass in a businesslike manner, seemingly content with their surroundings. This attitude of the quiet horses took some of the fear from Mustang.

At this moment the moon rose and Mustang could see everything around him in the place. The four heavy draft horses went on with their grazing as if they had always known what went on here and were quite

satisfied with it all. Mustang, by nature, was
not that kind of horse. He put his head down
to the grass and took a few mouthfuls, but
he found it impossible to be wholly at ease.
For a moment he stood looking at the long
line of a long, low-built structure to the west
of him. The longer he looked at it the more
interest it held for him, since his nose told
him there were horses inside that queer-look-
ing, very long, low building. He could not
see the horses inside, but he was near enough
so that he could not only scent them but he
could, now and then, hear them as they blew
through their nostrils, as a horse will do
when he is eating hay from a manger and
dust or something gets in his nose. All this
had a familiar sound to Mustang. He too,
when he was with Sam, had been in a stable
where he and Old Bill ate their hay and also
the delicious oats that Sam brought to them.
Mustang left the peaceful draft horses and
walked up close to the long line of stables.
When quite near he stopped and stood look-

ing, with the bright moon shining full upon him.

Mustang had no way of knowing, but he was on the edge of one of those unusually enterprising towns of the West. This town was already ahead of many of them, having a race track where horse races were held each fall, and throngs of people crowded the grandstand to watch the races. What Mustang saw here in the long, low building was a racing stable which, on this night, held many horses and the men to care for them who slept on bunks in the stable. None of the race horses, as they were known in these days, were full thoroughbreds, but all of them had racing stock in them and some of them had unusual speed.

At this time there were what were called "slick" men, those who understood this type of running horse. These "slick" men took these horses from town to town, with their fair grounds, and they knew that when the races came there would be many people there to see. This town, particularly, had an advantage in that there were troops of the U. S. Cavalry stationed a short distance away. On the days of the races many officers and men in their blue uniforms were present, and also many cattlemen and cowboys with their wide-brimmed hats and their ever-clinking spurs. These gave a color to the scene that the many boys of the town who always came to these races would not forget.

Mustang did not know all this as he stood in the moonlight and looked at the long line of stables before him. He turned his head and looked back at the work horses still feeding in the valley. Everything seemed to be peaceful about the place so that Mustang began to have little fear. He moved nearer to the racing stables, to satisfy his curiosity, when a delicious smell came to him. It was the smell of something good—the smell of oats. Mustang knew it was the same thing that Sam had so often put in the feed box at the Horseshoe Ranch. There is nothing a hungry horse likes better than oats and Mustang was no exception. All the horses in the line of stables just beyond him had their oats every day. In one of the empty stalls there were great sacks of oats piled high, sacks from which the horses had a short time before been fed. At this time they were all eating their oats, of which Mustang was well aware.

He felt a little suspicious of all these strange surroundings but the darkness around made him bold. The smell of the oats, the quiet of the horses in the stables, together with the steady grazing of the large work horses, now only a little behind him, made Mustang feel that he was safe enough to get some oats. He turned and, as if to look about the place, he walked in a circle once around the horses who were contentedly grazing. He even went up very close to the work horses but they paid no attention to him, going on with their grazing as if they did not see him. Mustang felt that he should have as little fear as they. Again he approached the line of racing stables and this time he boldly walked up to within a few feet of one of the stalls. As it happened he came up to a vacant stall, and the door was open.

Mustang stood for a brief time looking into the darkness of the stall. He could smell the oats in there and it seemed to him that it would be safe enough to venture a little more. He took a few steps forward, at the same time trying to see everything in the dark place. As he stood with his head inside the stall, the moonlight still fell full upon him.

It happened that at this moment one of the men who took care of the racing horses was standing in the shadows a short distance from the place. He saw Mustang standing and peering into the darkness of the vacant stall. Seeing the tall, rangy form of Mustang the shrewd man was at once interested. He remembered that a stable boy had put some oats in a feed box in the stall there and left the door open. And Mustang might go inside! Instantly the man who was experienced with racing horses began to scheme. He thought to himself that there was a remarkable horse if he could be caught! It came to him that the horse might have an owner about the place, but like as not he was one of those stray horses of the West that had escaped from some traveler. In any case, if he could catch this horse, he could talk the matter over with his associates later. If no one claimed the horse he would belong to the racing stables!

Mustang did not know all this as he took another step forward and put his head farther into the darkness of the stall. The man was watching him intently. There were two doors, an upper and a lower, on the stalls for the racing horses. The lower door was kept closed if there was a horse in the stall but the upper door was generally open, held back in place by a clever lock, so that this door would lock if slammed shut. Both doors always opened outward.

The man, peering from the shadows, saw that both doors were open at the stall where Mustang stood, each held back in place by an iron hook. If Mustang did go in the stall the man would have only to slip quickly down to the place, lift the iron hook on this side and shut the lower door and hook it to its staple just inside. The man had removed his boots and stood in his sock feet, for he had been on the point of going to bed. He would make no more sound than a cat in moving swiftly over the ground to reach the lower door if Mustang went in—and now he *did* go in! At this moment one of the big work horses walked up close to the stall and stood looking in. Mustang was eating big mouthfuls of the oats from the box. He turned his head once toward the open door and looked at the big horse who stood looking in, but the horse only made Mustang the more eager to eat the oats. Now the big horse came in and at the same time another was about to crowd in behind. Mustang drove them out and they both stood a little way off.

Mustang turned and looked behind him. The two big horses were still standing there looking at him eating the oats. Mustang understood and he ate without fear because it seemed to him that there was no one to watch him now but the two quiet horses standing there in the moonlight. He turned to his feed and had taken a big mouthful when he heard a sound behind him. He jerked his head up from the feed trough and looked back quickly toward the open door, and just as he looked he was startled to see the lower door go shut. As it did so he saw only the arm of a man move quickly above the door when he put the steel hook in its staple on the inside of the stall.

The man had sneaked alongside the stables in his sock feet and since the door was open, with the hook toward him, he was able to close the door quickly by bending low and still keep out of sight, all but his arm and hand. The next second the top door also went shut and the lock on that door clicked. This upper door, as mentioned, could be opened or shut from either side.

Mustang snorted, being fearful now that a man might appear, yet nothing happened. The two big horses had moved back a little but they had not been afraid of the man who closed the stall doors. There was a great difference between the feelings of Mustang and the two work horses standing quietly outside looking at the closed doors. Mustang knew that he had suddenly become a prisoner. They, on the contrary, could go about outside anywhere they chose. They seemed to be only mildly curious. One of them walked up to the closed doors, put his nose to it and smelled it for a little, then turned about, and he and the other horse walked off some distance and went on grazing as if nothing had happened. But Mustang only grew more concerned with his plight here.

When morning came the man who had shut the door on Mustang held a conversation with the owner of the racing horses. It was still four days until the horse races would begin on the track at the fair grounds. As a result of this conversation Pete, a small rider with narrow, black eyes and a continual grin on his face, was told to take full charge of Mustang during the next few days and to ride him in the forthcoming race.

Pete was pleased. He carefully opened the door to Mustang's stall and stood for a full minute studying him. At once he saw that Mustang did not have the angry, treacherous eyes of a broncho. He had large, dark eyes that showed both fear and wonder as he looked at Pete. And Pete noted that there was quite as much wonder in Mustang's dark eyes as fear. Pete began by talking quietly to him and he kept on talking while he edged alongside the stall and put a pail of oats in Mustang's feed box. Still talking softly to Mustang, Pete moved back and, after some time, he was pleased to see Mustang step to the feed box. He took a mouthful of the oats but turned and looked at Pete. Pete kept on talking to him. The result was that on the second day Pete was able to rub Mustang's neck while he ate his feed. After this the rider spent most of his time in the stable talking to Mustang, rubbing his neck and telling him that he would not be hurt in the least.

That afternoon Pete put a light racing saddle on Mustang and led him out to the edge of the race track. Pete mounted him and Mustang did not seem to be concerned. When his rider patted him gently on the neck and encouraged him to go forward Mustang at once complied. He walked through the opening of the low fence by the track. This fence was rather a flimsy one, not more than three feet high, made of small pine posts, on top of which were nailed long, narrow pine top rails. Pete rode Mustang out on the race track and Mustang did not try to buck, since the man had been gentle and kindly to him from the first. Pete leaned over and patted Mustang on the neck and made him know that he wanted him to gallop along the track. This was agreeable to Mustang, for he wanted exercise. He went forward in long, easy bounds and in this way he galloped twice clear around the mile track and Pete let him run the last time down the home stretch. Then Mustang was taken back to his stable and a blanket was put on him and he was led about the fair grounds to allow him to cool off gradually so as to be in good shape for the race.

The race track at this fair ground was unusual in that it was a mile track. Most of the race tracks of these days were but a half mile. There were only a few tracks that were a full mile around. A wealthy man by the name of Colonel John Manning had had the mile track made here. If the running race was to be only a half mile the horses were started at the half mile post on the far side of the track. Colonel Manning, himself, decided how far the horses should run. His word was final, since he owned the fair ground.

The Colonel had seen Mustang that evening as Pete walked him about on the grounds. The Colonel was surprised and delighted. He called to Pete, and said, "Such a magnificent horse! Such legs! Such a chest! Why, I'll bet he's got everything! Well, we shall see. This is to be a mile race, my man. Do you think the horse will give a good account of himself?"

"I am very sure he will, Colonel," said Pete with a grin, and he was delighted, for while he did not know for certain how much endurance Mustang had, he believed he had much and he was eager to see. Other men saw Mustang before the race and all sorts of bets were made. Some were that Mustang would win by a length over a long-legged sorrel mare that had the best racing blood in her. Some bet Mustang would win by two lengths, others that he would win only by a nose, while others, who had seen the long-legged mare run and win often, bet she would beat Mustang. And there were some who bet on a certain big bay horse and others on a dapple gray they had seen win races.

The day for the race came and as the hour approached the fair grounds were filled with hundreds of people.

Pete, who had taken care of Mustang, understood him and he was very careful with him on this day, for he doubted that Mustang had ever before run in such a race. Pete could see that with the power Mustang had in him he might get out of hand if he got frightened at seeing so many people.

Mustang was kept in his stall until an hour

before the race. Then Pete led him out behind the stables and walked him up and down to keep him limbered up, and during this time, Pete stopped now and then to pat Mustang on the neck and tell him that he need not get excited since all was well.

At last there sounded the clanging of the bell in the judges' stand at the race track, telling the riders of the horses that the judges were ready for the race. Pete, with a final pat on Mustang's neck, led him onto the fair ground, mounted him and rode forth toward the race track.

Already all the other horses with their riders were on the track moving about. Many of the horses were nervous and prancing— they knew they were soon to run with all their might around this track. The sorrel mare was dancing about on the track, nervous for the race, while both the big dapple gray and a big roan horse were whirling and plunging so much that it was difficult for their riders to keep them in hand. There were eight horses in all to run in this race.

A great shout went up from the crowd in the grandstand when Pete rode Mustang out on the track.

VII

MUSTANG'S rider urged him up the track toward the place where all the horses were to form in line, then turn and come down toward the wire for the start. The judges were in the stand above the starting place ready to shout "go!" when the horses reached the wire, unless some were too far ahead of the others.

As the horses started up the track to get ready for the race they were all, except Mustang, plunging and trying to whirl and run back. They knew from experience that they were to run a race and each horse wanted to get ahead of all the others. It seemed as if each horse was saying to his rider, "Let us turn about quickly, get a head start, and have this race all over with!"

Mustang began to feel a little nervous, but he kept calm because Pete, his rider, bent low and patted him on the neck almost constantly as he spoke low to him, saying, "It's all right. Don't get scared. It's all right." Mustang did not understand the words, but the tone of the voice and the gentle pats on his neck somehow reassured him. He watched the other horses dancing and whirling around him. Once the long-legged sorrel mare whirled and jostled against him. The dapple gray horse was constantly trying to get out of hand and so get the lead, and once he leaped aside so quickly that he struck Mustang hard on the hip, but Mustang only danced forward a little. None of the riders wore spurs in these races, but all of them carried short whips, except Pete. He cleverly guessed he would need no whip and as he looked at Mustang moving along with his head high, watching the antics of the other horses, Pete said aloud to him, "I guess they all act pretty crazy to you. Each one of them thinks he'll win this race, but you and I'll see about that!"

The grandstand was now full of people and many boys and men stood close to the low fence for a considerable distance on each side of the grandstand. There were also many soldiers with their blue uniforms and many cowboys with their broad-brimmed hats, high-heeled boots and clanking spurs. All the people were joking and laughing and all were eager for the race to start.

The fair ground was surrounded by a high, tight board fence with two wide gates where men stood to take the tickets from persons coming in. One of these wide openings was in a line beyond the wire, where the horses must finish the race. Well up the track Mustang was allowed to turn. As he looked down the track he saw the grandstand and things in general. He saw the opening in the high board fence where, at the moment, a man was leading two work horses outside the fair ground. Mustang had felt a little nervous from the time Pete mounted him and rode him out on the race track with the other horses. The only reason he had not thrown Pete off was because the man had been gentle with him, but all the same Mustang felt restless. Pete patted him and talked to him while Mustang stood for a little and gazed down the track toward the opening in the fence.

Suddenly Mustang gave a start. He heard the sharp clanging of the bell in the judges' stand. This was the signal for the men who were riding the horses to get them in hand and start down the track toward the wire for the race. At this moment all the horses began to leap and plunge to go faster and each rider was trying his best to outdo the others so as to get the head start when they reached the wire. Down the track at a gallop they all came, Mustang with them. Some of the horses almost got out of hand. The long-

legged mare was almost as cunning as her
rider. She had already got out ahead of the
others and her rider acted as if he were holding her back because he knew that if she got
too far out in front the judges would call
them all back to start over. The judges, however, could not be fooled. The tall roan horse
and the dapple gray were close upon the
mare while the other horses, except Mustang, were coming down the track bunched
together. Mustang's rider kept him on the
outside of all the others so as to keep him as
calm as possible. Having the outside track
was a disadvantage in that a horse would have
to run in a bigger circle than those on the inside, but the rider on Mustang was confident.

In these days of racing it was often difficult to get the horses off to a fair start. The
reason was that as the horses all came galloping down toward the starting point, each
rider tried to get a little ahead of the others,
with the result that some horses at the start
were too far ahead. That was how it was on

this first attempt at a start here. All the horses, except Mustang, had run in races before and most of them were as anxious to get the advantage at the start as their riders were. The horses, champing at their bits, came galloping down toward the wire, but the rider on the long-legged mare let her out so fast that she was several lengths ahead for the start. The bell clanged in the judges' stand, which meant that the start was not fair, and the riders had to pull up their nervous horses when well down the track and ride back for another attempt. One of the judges reprimanded the rider of the mare for his action and cautioned him lest he be disqualified.

Mustang was now getting scared and he leaped and plunged so much that he seemed to be getting out of hand. He was afraid and nervous because the whole thing was so strange to him. He was afraid of the crowd of people in the grandstand and also the long lines of people standing near the low fence on either side of the place. He had never seen anything like it. The only thing that now kept him from rushing away from all this was the man on his back who never ceased talking to him and patting his neck. Not once had Mustang been hurt and the kindly action of this man still kept him on the track with the other horses.

As Mustang moved back past the great crowd of people he was the center of attraction. Men yelled their admiration. "Look at that big bay with the white stocking legs! He's got it in him!"

"You bet he has! Look at that chest! He's got speed and bottom, too!"

"It's so! He's not only a mile horse—he's a *ten*-mile horse if it comes to that!"

"That's it, if he gets half a chance he'll beat the field!"

"That's so! He's a natural!"

A veteran soldier yelled, "He's like General Grant—bothered only until he can begin —then he'll win!"

Loud shouts of approval greeted this from other still young Civil War veterans who sat near. They shouted, "Hurrah for that big bay with the white stocking legs! He'll win."

Some of the men knew Pete who rode Mustang and they began to shout, "That's right, Pete, keep that big horse quiet, then when the race starts he'll show 'em!"

The tall, slim cowboys stood by the fence looking on. They joked and shouted at Mustang's rider, "Be sure to set up in the middle of that horse, Pete! Otherwise he might get tired and set down on you!"

Pete seemed not to hear the jokes of the cowboys. He knew them and was used to their talk. As he rode up the track and near the cowboys Mustang saw the men in the wide-brimmed hats, and as two of them moved up along the fence the small "bells" on their spurs jingled. Mustang snorted and shied away. He remembered it was men like these cowboys who had got on his back and gouged his sides with those jingling, cutting things. Pete saw Mustang was afraid of the cowboys but he did not understand the cause. All he knew was that Mustang, for some reason, seemed more afraid of the cowboys than the other men standing alongside the fence by the track.

The horses were now well up the track and again the clanging bell in the judges' stand told the riders that they must turn and come back down the track to get a fair start at the wire. At the clanging of the bell the riders turned their horses and down the track they came. A light shower of rain had fallen the day before and there was scarcely any dust made by the horses' flying hoofs. Each rider held his horse back this time and as the horses came on it was seen that the race was to begin.

Mustang had been a little slow as Pete let him have his head. By chance he was next to the outside horse, and as he and this horse were a little behind all the others and they came neck and neck under the wire, the judges shouted "go!" It was a fair enough start.

At the word "go!" the long-legged mare shot out ahead of the field and there were wild yells from the great crowd watching. The horses were all running near each other —the mare ahead—when they reached the first quarter-mile pole, but when they passed that the mare began to draw away while the dapple gray steadily began to draw nearer to her from the rear. All these skilled riders knew that a running race of a mile was a long one and each rider tried to use great care so that his horse did not overdo in the beginning.

At this point Mustang, by the constant light slapping of Pete's hand, seemed to understand something of what was wanted. He was running in long, powerful leaps but running easily. When Pete slapped him with his palm and called to him to go faster Mustang understood. He leaped forward, passed two horses and was close upon the dapple gray, with the mare two lengths ahead.

A wild yell of admiration from the people in the grandstand greeted Mustang's new burst of speed. Mustang passed a big bay and crowded close to the dapple gray and again wild yells came from the grandstand. The rider on the mare looked back, scared. He struck the mare with his whip and she shot ahead of Mustang three lengths. On they raced, and on to the three-quarter pole—and now the home stretch!

The people in the grandstand were on their feet. Pete slapped Mustang on the neck with the palm of his hand and now, for the first time, shouted loudly at him to go faster. Mustang understood. He must really run now! He must run past the mare! He leaped forward and for the first time he extended himself. He leaped like a hound and, running to one side of the mare, he was almost even when the rider of the mare began to ply his whip to her with all his power. The mare gave all she had but Mustang shot past her, and down the home stretch he came like a thunderbolt — one length — two — three lengths ahead of the mare and all the field.

Pandemonium broke loose among the crowd. Wild yells came from the cowboys as Mustang raced under the wire, then the sound of shooting from the cowboys' big revolvers, and this, with all the shouting and yelling, made Mustang terror-stricken. Down the track he ran with all his might, and seeing the wide open space in the tall fence beyond, he leaped aside so swiftly that Pete, even though he was a good rider, was thrown. Mustang jumped the low fence beside the track and raced toward the open gate. Two men out that way tried to turn him back by running toward him, waving their hats and yelling at him, but they had to jump aside or Mustang would have run over them. Out of the fair ground gate he ran and on across the open plain, the bridle and the light saddle still on him. Mustang was headed north.

The crowd forgot everything now but the sight of this magnificent horse running away. Pete, who had been thrown on the track, got up, unhurt. When he saw Mustang rushing toward the gate he yelled loudly for help, shouting, "He'll run clear away—stop him!" But even before this the men were seen running toward their horses, standing saddled and bridled at a long hitching rack some distance toward the stables. A closed gate was now swung open on the side of the fair ground toward the north. The riders all rode their horses at a run out of this gate and headed toward Mustang who had turned and was now running toward the northwest.

When he realized all the horsemen were coming toward him he took one quick look at them, then turned and ran straight into the west. To do this he was at some disadvantage, for a short distance ahead there was a small stream bordered by tangled thickets of brush and low trees. Mustang ran hard, crashed through the brush, splashed across the shallow water to a broad, grassy plain beyond.

By this time other riders on swift horses were running along a rise of ground to the south of Mustang, their purpose being to turn him back so that the first group of riders might get close to him with their ropes. These men urged their horses on so fast that Mustang was compelled to veer a little which brought him nearer four riders at that point. These men raced in hard to turn Mustang. But he ran in a surprising burst of speed and all at once he was running free and alone, swiftly increasing the distance between him and his pursuers.

On and on he ran. When night fell Mustang found himself on a wide plain, thickly covered with buffalo grass. For the first time he felt himself free from the men and he began to graze. He was bothered in his grazing because of the iron bridle bit in his mouth. After much practice a horse could graze and chew grass with a bridle bit in his mouth, but it was always troublesome. When Mustang put his head down to graze the short bridle rein dropped over one ear and lay against the other. He flicked the ear to free it from the strap and, by chance, the reins fell to the ground. Mustang went on grazing and presently, although he did not know, he stepped with a front foot on the dragging reins. Seeing a dark form moving across the plain ahead of him he threw up his head to look, his front hoof still on the rein. The result was that his head had come up only a short distance when he felt the jerk of the bridle on his head. A little scared, he jerked hard. There was no strap on the bridle under his throat, as there were on some. He jerked again, his front hoof still standing on the bridle rein. At this second hard jerk the bridle was pulled over his head and the whole thing, including the troublesome iron bit, dropped at his feet.

Mustang looked at the moving animal again. It was a coyote, and when he saw that it ran on he gave a snort and again went on grazing. He could now eat the grass easily and as rapidly as he wished. He was wholly free except for the light racing saddle on his back. In the bright starlight he grazed here for some time and then quenched his thirst at a nearby pool of water.

It was nearly midnight when he raised his head and looked all around him, feeling comfortable in every way except that there was an itching on his back where he felt the saddle. Like horses in general, when Mustang's back or sides itched, he relieved himself by lying down and rolling. He decided to indulge himself in this comfort and at once dropped down on the buffalo sod and began to roll. Some horses can roll clear over and so roll from one side to another and scratch themselves all they wish at the first lying down. Most horses, however, have to get to their feet after scratching one side, then lie down on the other side. When Mustang was a year old he could **roll clear** over and Sam

McSwain had noticed this and grinned with pleasure. Mustang now rolled on one side for a minute and then, with an effort, whirled to roll over on the other side. But the light saddle caught on the sod the first time and prevented Mustang from rolling clear over. He tried again and he exerted himself vigorously. The result was that by this effort the saddle was turned so that it rested on his side. Feeling that he had made some headway in moving the thing he rolled clear over on that side and he felt the saddle under him. It pressed against him and annoyed him. He stretched his head out and scratched his neck on the grass, while moving his hind legs in every way he could, trying to rub the saddle off. It was still there but the girth was loose and he had now worked it along his body so that when he finally got to his feet the saddle dropped under him with the girth on the root of his tail. Instinctively he reared and plunged forward, and the girth slid over his tail and dropped on his hocks. At once he began kicking and both saddle and girth fell to the ground. Mustang kicked again to be sure the thing was off, then he turned, put his head down toward the saddle on the grass and snorted as if it had been a thing alive.

He was wholly free now and he had a feeling that he wanted to move. He leaped away at a gallop across the buffalo grass toward the southwest. As he traveled he was uncertain and suspicious, but he wanted to keep going.

VIII

MUSTANG had no plan in his wandering. He simply traveled where he found the best grass and where there were vast stretches of wild plains and hills that offered him freedom.

The autumn passed and winter came, but Mustang was south of the colder ranges in the north. All through December, January and February he wandered in a region where he found the days and nights cold, but this winter less snow than usual had fallen, and the life-giving buffalo grass was everywhere.

Several times during the winter months he came upon small herds of wild horses led by their ever-present stallions, all of which were much smaller than Mustang. The stallions, in every instance, showed that they looked on Mustang as a horse that had no business in their vicinity, and they would run at him to drive him away. Mustang, however, had a different opinion about the matter. He would wait calmly until the stallion came up, then he would whirl and let the stallion have the full power of his hoofs in the ribs. One full strike of Mustang's hoofs was enough. The stallion would run off a distance and snort in fear.

There were other wild horses to the north and west of this place and among them were some bigger wild stallions, the kind that cattlemen said "would plumb eat up" a gelding unless he was a big one and the kind that would fight back. But it didn't matter what kind of horse came at him, if the horse wanted to fight, Mustang would, as the western men said, "get plumb tough on that horse and discourage that horse complete." Mustang still wanted the companionship of other horses, but since the wild horses were never sociable with him he did not let them bother him. At the end of a year here on his own, he was almost like the wild horses themselves. When he found they did not want him around he stood his ground nevertheless.

One day Mustang was grazing on an unusually good stretch of green grass when he saw a small herd of wild horses, led by a stallion, coming toward him. The stallion, it seemed, had decided that he would take over this good grass here, but Mustang went on grazing until the stallion came at him with bared teeth. Mustang rushed at the enemy and attacked him like a wildcat. He got a hold with his long teeth, and the small but tough stallion broke free and ran, the other wild ones with him. Mustang stood and looked at them for a little time while they circled toward the west, running and snorting.

At this time Mustang saw only the wild horses running and he did not know that human eyes saw him when he drove the stallion away. Yet there were two men who saw it all. These men, both top riders, were cronies and were known to the ranchmen as Jim and Link. They were skilled in catching wild horses and when they saw Mustang they at once recognized in him a horse of rare beauty and power. Knowing the region well here they knew Mustang was a newcomer. And to them he was a stray horse and one that would be valuable if they could catch him.

Link and Jim were hidden in a clump of trees when they saw Mustang drive the wild stallion away. They now kept still as they sat on their horses watching him. Mustang, unmindful that human eyes were upon him, went on grazing for a time, then he raised his head and looked across the plain. Link and Jim saw him walk toward a water hole that lay at the foot of a steep rise of ground, but he stopped and looked toward the west. Jim and Link turned their eyes in that direction. They saw a small herd of wild horses

coming over a rise of ground. When the
horses got close to the water hole they
stopped and looked at Mustang, then moved
up to the water and spent some time drinking.
Mustang walked up to the water and the
wild ones showed their displeasure by laying
back their ears and coming at him. There
was some squealing and kicking while Mustang let them know that the water here was
his as much as theirs and in quick time they
found he was too tough for them. They
moved away a little and looked at him while
he drank, then they started back in the direction they had come from. Mustang decided
he wanted horse company, and followed
them.

Link and Jim watched until all the horses,
including Mustang, had disappeared. Then
they rode up to the big water hole. This was
a familiar place to them. They tied their
horses to a small tree and stood beside a wild
horse trap they had made a year before. This
trap was a hole they had dug, large enough

to hold a big wild stallion, a hole they had cleverly covered at the time with limbs and brush found near the place. The hole had been dug in the middle of the trail leading to the water, and Link and Jim had hoped that in time the big stallion they were trying to get might be in a hurry for water and walk into it. But the wild one was too clever, as were all the other wild horses. But Link and Jim were as patient as the wild things themselves. They would fix the old trap again and try for Mustang.

At the bottom of these wild horse traps there was much loose, soft earth so that a horse was almost never injured by his fall into the hole. This was so of the trap being fixed now for Mustang. He would be terribly scared by his fall but he wouldn't be hurt.

Two old spades had been left here by the men when they quit work the year before, and these could be used now if needed. This was a dry country where little rain fell and the hole was about the same as when they had dug it last year. But they worked carefully to cover the hole which they hoped Mustang would fall into.

The men talked while they worked. Jim said, "Link, I don't believe that big bay is a wild horse. He acts to me like a stray tame horse."

"That's so," Link said, "and the wild ones don't seem to like him. They want to fight him and drive him away, but no matter if he is a tame horse, if we can get him we'll have a horse that'll bring us money."

"You bet he will," Jim said, "that is, if anybody can ride him. Say, if we do get him, I bet he'll make an awful fight. It'll be awful hard to set up in the middle of him!"

Link and Jim were among the best of riders. They would try to ride any horse, but they knew that a big, powerful horse like Mustang, if he fought, could buck twice as hard and throw a rider twice as hard as a small horse. But there were two of them and with their skill and their ropes they were more than willing to try Mustang if they could capture him. They knew the range horses for miles around and they knew that while Mustang must have been owned by someone he was a newcomer here. Being adventurous men, like others of their kind, they would take chances on keeping Mustang if they could catch him. If there was a brand on him they knew they could change it and they thought but little about that part of the matter.

Link and Jim spread brush over the old poles that still lay across the hole and they worked most of the day to complete the trap for Mustang. They were wise enough to know he would not walk right into such a trap. Even a horse that had been raised with men had some instincts that warned him. The plan of Jim and Link was well laid. They had in their minds that if Mustang should walk close to the hole, they would rush out and frighten him suddenly so that he would leap aside to get away and so leap fairly on the treacherous covering of the trap and crash down through the dead limbs and brush. They knew if he did this they would have to throw a rope over his head at once and then dig a slope so that he might plunge up and out.

As they worked they stopped often to look out across the plain to see if there was any sign of Mustang. But they did not see him or any of the wild ones. They saw nothing of life all day except, now and then, a few crows that flew to the ground not far away to watch them.

Link and Jim knew the habits of the wild horses and they knew that, unlike the range or tame horses, the wild ones could, and did, go two or three days without water if there was too much danger in getting to it. But range or tame horses would hunt water at least once or twice each day in the summer. The men believed that Mustang would come back to the water hole during the coming night since water was scarce in this region.

Link said, after he had wiped the sweat from his face, "Jim, it's a pretty warm day. Looks like that big bay horse might want water again by evening. What do you think?"

Jim said, "I think he will. He'll come, but I hope he don't come back till it's dark. If the wind stays right and everything is quiet around here we ought to have a good chance of hiding and scaring him when he comes to drink so he'll jump aside and fall in this hole before he knows it."

The water hole was near a hollow that cut its way back a little into a steep bank some six feet high. Link and Jim planned to have their horses tied there so that they might lure Mustang on. They knew the nature of horses and they were certain that Mustang would be interested in seeing the two horses standing tied there, and if the wind was right for the purpose, as it was now, Mustang might be curious enough to forget everything except the two horses. And if the horses should nicker in a friendly way to him he would be very likely to come up close to them. But Link and Jim wanted him to come along the trail so that he would stand close beside the trap they had fixed for him. They would be hiding behind a big mass of boulders close by.

The time passed, evening came, and the night fell quickly. The sky was clear and the stars were shining, and Link and Jim noticed that the breeze was still blowing steadily from the west. This seemed just right. Mustang, when they last saw him, was going in that direction and they believed he would come back from the same direction. Accordingly, they brought up their horses and tied them to the tree selected, and then they hid behind the tall mass of rocks. Now it seemed to them that if Mustang came up to the water hole they could carry out their plan. But they knew their timing must be perfect. They must both leap out and rush at him when he was just beside trap. They did not expect him to walk directly into the covered hole, but as the wild horse trail led alongside, it seemed natural that he would follow this trail as he had done in the morning.

Jim and Link had removed their hats and they sat on the ground where they could peer around the mass of big rocks. An hour of the night passed. All at once the wind blew stronger. It whispered through the spaces in the mass of boulders and blew on the faces of the men. They were pleased with the stiffening breeze. They knew this would keep the man smell away from Mustang if he came up the wind and they believed he would, considering the direction he had gone. But if Mustang should happen to come up over the high ground beyond where the two horses were tied, that would ruin their chances of getting him. Now and then the men turned their heads and looked above their horses toward the skyline beyond, but there was no sign of life up there—nothing but the silence and the night sky with the stars shining. On the plain toward the west they could see, here and there, a lone tree that stood out like a dark sentinel in the night. Once they saw two small shadowy forms move close together near a tree, then stop, and for a time they could not be seen in the shadows. Link and Jim were sure they were coyotes and there was nothing about them that would scare a horse.

As the two men settled down into complete silence for a minute, they saw something moving toward them along the ground in the starlight, a wriggling form that they at once recognized as a big snake. It kept coming on until it was but a short distance from the pile of boulders. When it saw the men it instantly coiled, with its head up, and they heard the dull, buzzing sound made by its tail, uplifted from its coil.

Jim whispered, "A rattlesnake, Link. We got to get rid of him!"

While the snake rattled and threatened, Jim crawled a little away and picked up a long dead stick. When he returned, Link was ready with a stone in his hand. "All right!"

Jim whispered and Link threw the stone at the snake, striking it fair. While it flopped about Jim struck it quickly several times with the stick and killed it. He reached out with the stick and flipped the snake some distance away.

The two saddle horses, tied to the tree, snorted and moved about in their fear of the rattler, but when Jim and Link resumed their watch for Mustang the horses soon got quiet and stood with heads raised, gazing out on the shadowy plain beyond, not knowing why their riders still waited and, now and then, moved so stealthily beside the big pile of rocks.

There was a hollow out on the plain not far from a low, brushy thicket. It happened that both Jim and Link were looking out in that direction when they saw the form of a big, tall horse appear as he came out of the hollow and on past the brushy thicket, where he stood in full view. It was Mustang. For a few seconds he stood looking in this direc-

tion, then he came forward at a walk, moving
toward the pool of water. As he came nearer
Link and Jim could hear the thumping
sounds of his big hoofs on the sod and as he
walked nearer still they heard him give a low
snort which told them he was suspicious and
that he would advance cautiously. He stopped
when a little nearer and stood with his head
up, looking at the two horses by the tree beyond the pool of water.

After a little time all seemed well to Mustang and, being very thirsty, he walked slowly
up along the trail toward the pool. As he did
so one of the saddle horses tied there reassured him by whinnying in a friendly manner. For the moment he forgot all but his
thirst. It seemed to him that in the night here
he might go up to the pool and drink. There
was the good hard ground of the trail leading past the brush-covered hole and being a
tame horse, Mustang did not suspect anything wrong here. In fact he paid but little
attention to the brush-covered place except

that he expected to pass by and at once reach
the water. The stiff wind prevented him getting the least hint of men nearby. He walked
on.

When he was just where the men wanted
him, both Jim and Link rushed out from
each end of the rock pile, yelling at him. In
his first wild fright Mustang leaped sidewise
with all his might to escape the two men who
were almost upon him. He crashed down into
the hole. At the same time an astonishing
thing happened to Jim. As he rushed forward
he stumbled on a stone, pitched headlong,
and, to his consternation, he fell into the hole
beside Mustang! Jim got to his feet in the
hole and without a sound coming from him,
he stood close against the steep side of the
trap.

Link saw Jim's danger. He moved farther
back so as not to excite Mustang and called
softly, "Keep still, Jim. Don't move!" And
Jim, filled with fear, kept still.

Mustang snorted loudly once, then stood

trembling. His head and the upper part of his neck to his withers protruded above the hole. It would have been easy for Link to throw a loop over Mustang's head now, but this would have been dangerous since Mustang might begin kicking and fatally injure Jim, or even trample him to death.

Link had not yet seen Jim since he fell in the hole. He called softly, "Jim, if you are on your feet put a hand up so I can see. I'll get a rope to you in a minute." Jim crowded as close as he could to the side of the hole, and slowly straightened up. Link saw Jim's hand come up slowly toward the rear of Mustang, but Mustang was looking at Link who stood a little distance forward talking to him in low, soothing words.

Link knew Jim was on his feet when he saw his hand. He was glad Jim could stand and did not seem injured. Link slowly sat down on the ground in front and to one side of Mustang and kept on talking to him. Link's plan was to be so quiet and easy he could crawl up to the hole and pull Jim out, but he must be extremely careful. If he scared Mustang he might begin thrashing about in the hole. If Mustang should start plunging Link would have to rush up any-way and try to get hold of Jim's wrists and pull him up. The danger in this would be that Jim might be crushed or trampled be-fore Link could get hold of him. Jim knew this and he knew that Link knew. And he knew that Link was thinking fast while he sat there talking in low, soothing words to Mustang.

The effect of a man not moving and talk-ing quietly to him had a queer effect on Mus-tang. He had known kind treatment from some men who had got their hands on him and he knew he was helpless here. Up to now he had not been hurt and the longer the man sat and talked the more Mustang wanted to be quiet.

The moon arose above a ridge on the east and shone down on the scene. Mustang moved a little and his side pressed slightly against Jim. As Mustang turned his head a little, Jim could see his ears. Mustang did not set his ears stiffly forward as a horse would that was wild with fear. They moved alternately back and forth, and to Jim, the experienced horseman, this kind of movement of a horse's ears meant that the low, soothing words of Link were somewhat reassuring, and he was inclined to be calm here. If Link could come around behind Mustang he might run up quickly and get hold of Jim's hands and pull him up. This was in Link's mind now. He got on his hands and knees to start crawling around to the rear, but Mustang snorted at the move. Link got still again. Then he said softly, "Jim, rub him a little. If he starts jumping I'll run up and get hold of your hand. Keep one hand up on top while you rub him." Mustang's body was already against Jim. Slowly he rubbed him. Mustang did not flinch but turned his head a little and looked at Jim standing against the side of the hole.

Mustang's ears kept moving back and forth, and for a little time he simply stood looking while Jim kept rubbing but did not make a sound. Then came a remarkable thing. Mustang heaved a long breath. It was the kind of deep breath that told both men, who knew horses, that here was a horse that was not only a tame one but one with unusual intelligence. And that long breath from Mustang made Link and Jim understand that he had known good treatment at the hands of men and he was beginning to trust them here to help him. Link said softly, as Jim kept rubbing him, "Jim, I'm going to try to get around behind him and get hold of you."

Link stood up and moved slowly back to the saddle horses. He untied one of them that he could trust to stand, led it up slowly to a point not far from Mustang and tied it to a small bush. Mustang looked at the horse in front of him, and when the horse, with his head down, made a low, friendly sound, that helped. Link walked in a wide circle and came up behind the pile of boulders. Here he lay down and slowly wormed his way toward the rear of Mustang. Jim was still rubbing Mustang gently and his body still pressed a little against Jim. Mustang made no sound, but the flicker of his ears showed he was interested in the horse standing in front and still making friendly sounds to him, and he did not notice Jim in the rear.

At last Jim felt Link's hand. Link got a grip on Jim's wrist. When Link got that sure hold he knew he could do the rest. He got to his feet and pulled hard. Mustang snorted and crowded close against the other side of the hole. Link gripped both of Jim's wrists like a vise and pulled him up and out while Mustang snorted and still crowded the other side.

Both men, relieved to have that over, stood looking down on Mustang. They were proud to think that they had trapped him in this way, although they knew that chance had a lot to do with it. But the hole had been fixed just right and covered cleverly with brush and they had both jumped out from their hiding place just at the right instant. And the wind had been in their favor and against Mustang.

Suddenly the same thought came to Jim and Link. For a year both of them had worked for Sam McSwain on the Horseshoe Ranch, and they had seen and known Mustang when he was the favorite of Sam and all the men at the ranch. Link said, "Jim, we must be crazy. I bet anything this is Sam's horse, Mustang! Why didn't we think of this when we first saw him? But I guess it's because he was so far from home."

"I'll bet he *is* Mustang," said Jim. "*I* wonder, too, why we didn't think of it when we first saw him! You remember how much sense that Mustang horse had. The fellers at the Horseshoe all said he had more sense than any horse they'd ever seen and he was the

kind that trusted fellers, too. Well, well, and
look at what we've done to him here. Makes
a feller feel lower than a skunk! Well, let's
get them two old rusty spades and get him
out."

And so instead of hoping they had caught
a fine horse for themselves, they now felt
they had got Sam's horse, Mustang, and they
wanted to take him back to the Horseshoe
Ranch. They had not as yet been able to look
for a brand. Suddenly Mustang tried to rear
up. His knees struck the front of the hole
and stopped him but he reared again and got
his front feet up on the sod above. Frightened, he stood there. Quickly Link struck a
match and held it close. The flash of the
lighted match made the men exclaim, "It's
the Horseshoe brand and it *is* Mustang!"
Mustang was startled at the flash of the
match but he still stood on his hind legs with
his front feet on the ground above. Link and
Jim began calling him by his name and talking to him as if he were at home.

"Now, Mustang, we don't aim to hurt you!"

"If we had knowed it was you, we wouldn't have done such as this."

"Too bad Sam ain't here! *Wouldn't* he be glad we found you! Now we'll get a rope on you and get you out!"

"Now, be quiet. Just stand there nice like, where you are!"

"We'll tie a rope easy and gentle around your neck so it won't slip and choke you. We sure ain't going to throw a loop on you and choke you, not by a considerable, we ain't!"

Jim picked up one of the ropes. In the excitement of finding Mustang, he didn't notice which one it was, but by chance it was a rope that had been used many seasons. And a rope was supposed to be good until it broke. Mustang stood and trembled while Jim tied the rope around his neck. He still stood with his forefeet up on the top of the trap. He did not seem to want to drop back into the hole. He was this far up and he wanted to hold that advantage.

Jim took the saddle horse back to the other one. He tied the end of the long rope, that was now on Mustang's neck, to one of the boulders close to the ground. The rock would hold. Then Link and Jim worked carefully with the spades that had been left for such a time as this when a horse should be caught. They talked in low voices as they dug the earth away to let it fall in the hole so that Mustang would have a slope he could climb up. When they started digging in front of him, Mustang dropped back with all four feet in the hole.

Now and then the spades loosened a big chunk of earth that rolled down and struck Mustang on his hoofs. Each time he would jump when the earth struck him and, not knowing what it all meant, he only got more scared. Link and Jim worked slowly and occasionally they stopped and looked at Mustang in the moonlight.

As the loosened dirt rolled down in front of Mustang, they talked to him and they talked of Sam and the others at the Horseshoe Ranch. They speculated on the reason Mustang had left Sam at the ranch and agreed that he would not have gone away on his own account. Jim said, "Some horse thieves got him, I bet, and he got away from 'em all. Mustang wouldn't have left Sam except he was made to. Sam and Mustang was awful good friends."

At this instant one of the saddle horses, tied to the tree, snorted wildly and sprang as far as his rope would let him. At the same time Link and Jim heard the weird, deadly, buzzing rattle of what they knew was another rattlesnake. "Get a rock, Link," Jim said. They moved up near the horse and saw the rattler coiled. The rock and Jim's spade quickly did the work. Link lifted the killed snake on the spade and in disgust threw it away, saying, "Daggone these snakes, Jim, they generally keep quiet at night. I reckon

this was the mate to the other one. Rattle-
snakes is plumb disgusting and this one has
got Mustang all stirred up again."

Unfortunately this was true. Mustang
snorted and crowded around in his narrow
quarters, but instead of trying to rear up
again he crowded to the back end of the trap.
He was scared, as were the other horses.
Their snorting told him there had been
danger close by and Mustang was all the
more scared because he was helpless here in
this hole. When Jim and Link came up again
and started digging the dirt loose Mustang
quit snorting but looked at them with frightened eyes.

As Jim and Link worked their talk was
again about Mustang and Sam McSwain.
They knew it was a long way to the Horseshoe Ranch and they talked about how they
would get Mustang to Sam. Jim said, "Link,
we know Mustang's broke to a rope and if we
keep his rope tied to the saddle horn on one

of our horses, I reckon he'll come along without much fuss."

Link replied, "Maybe he will, but he's been a long time among strangers and us trapping him in this hole won't make him feel he can trust us any too much. He may give us trouble."

Link and Jim stopped work and looked down upon Mustang. Jim said, "Now ain't he a big horse, big and tall, and stronger than any steer. When we get it so he can get out of here he may come out like a shot. He's got the power if he wants to use it. Now ain't it too bad Sam ain't here. If Sam was here he could rub Mustang's nose a little and set right up on his back and ride him when he comes up out of this hole. And Sam could ride him all day with nothing on him at all, just tap him on the neck and turn him like we have seen him do many times."

"It's so," said Link. "I don't think it matters what fellers has had Mustang or how hard they have treated him. If Sam was to

come up to Mustang *anywhere,* Mustang
would be to Sam the same horse he was when
he and Sam were together. They sure did
seem to understand each other. But Sam
ain't here and when Mustang comes out of
here we may find we've got a wild outlaw
horse on our hands, but we got the rope on
his neck and we got it tied to a rock, so I
guess we'll hold him."

Link and Jim had already dug in front of
Mustang, and now they were so busy digging
the dirt and letting it fall into the hole from
the rear, so that Mustang could back up and
get a good start to plunge up and out, that
they did not stop to consider when he would
make up his mind to do this. But Mustang
was doing his own thinking about it. He kept
feeling the dirt falling in behind him and
several times he stepped back and up onto
some of the dirt so that the front of the hole,
with the slope now in front, was a little
farther from him. All at once he plunged up
and out of the hole. Link and Jim dropped

their spades and ran to the rock where the rope was tied to see that it didn't slip off. Mustang, in his fright, ran past the mass of boulders and against the rope. The force jerked him around hard. Wild now with fear, he lunged back with all his might. The rope on his neck broke and he fell back on his haunches. But he sprang to his feet instantly and ran with all his might. Astonished, Jim and Link stood watching him thundering across the plain in the moonlight.

Presently Jim said, "Well, Link, Mustang's headed toward the southwest and that's the direction of the Almazan Ranch. There's lots of other horses on the range there. Maybe he'll get in that territory and stay there until we can get to Sam and tell him."

They stood for a while and talked together. It would take some time for them to ride to the distant ranch and tell Sam the news. They knew that as soon as Sam heard he would mount and ride in search of his horse. Link and Jim, like all the men at the

Horseshoe, would be very glad if Sam could get this great bay horse back home again. They mounted and started their tough, wiry horses at a trot toward the far distant Horseshoe Ranch.

IX

WHEN Mustang escaped from Link and Jim he didn't move along any particular course. It happened, however, that he wandered toward the south and west, although this came about simply because he wanted to get as far from those men as possible. He had nothing more in mind at this time.

So it was that Mustang traveled over the plains country for several weeks. One day he saw a herd of wild horses grazing on a rich green plain near some cottonwood trees. He had met such creatures before and he knew now they were not the kind he would enjoy being with. He wanted tame horses for company because they were like him. But he felt

180

this grass out here was as much his as the
wild horses'. And after grazing some time
Mustang left them and traveled on alone.

During these days he saw herds of cattle,
and one day when he came up suddenly on a
high hill he saw two men riding below in a
deep valley. As soon as he saw them, he
whirled and ran. Mustang felt now that he
would rather live all alone than allow any
man whatever to get hold of him.

One afternoon he arrived at a long slough
filled with tall dead grass and brush as high
as his neck. He avoided the tall brush and
walked on the plain nearby, and as he moved
he kept looking forward toward a place
where a line of high bluffs arose from the
broad plain not far beyond. Mustang stood
looking toward the point where the hill arose
from the plain, then he went on again. Once
he stopped and listened. He heard sounds
somewhere beyond the hill and he was curious. Suddenly he whirled and ran back into
the marsh, where he stood watching, only his

head and neck showing above the tall slough grass and brush.

From around the hill three horses came running and behind them were three men on horses. He saw the riders race over the plain and turn the horses back, then they all disappeared around the bluff, leaving only a little dust that had been stirred up by the running horses. But sounds still came to Mustang—sounds that made him understand that men were riding on the other side of the high bluff beyond.

Some minutes passed and Mustang again saw running horses. This time there were two of them who ran out from behind the tall bluff, but they had no sooner come in sight than the hard-riding men rode in front of them and they all turned and disappeared behind the hill as did those before. Mustang did not know what it all meant but he knew that the riders somehow were controlling the horses they chased. He stood in his hiding place for a little time, and then he boldly walked out in the open and stood majestically, looking. He was a horse striking to look at as he stood here, his bright bay coat glistening in the sunlight, the big white spot on his chest, and his four trim white stocking legs showing beautifully against the green plain where he stood.

Mustang could hear the sounds on the other side of the bluff as he stood looking but he could see neither a horse nor a man on the plain. Then, all at once, he *did* see something at the foot of the bluff. It seemed, at first, to be only the hind part of a horse, but it disappeared and again he saw something move. It moved beside a clump of bushes at the foot of the bluff. As Mustang stood looking at it he recognized the head of a man, a man with a wide-brimmed hat.

This man was none other than Sam McSwain, out here on this day with the men of the Horseshoe Ranch to round up some range horses for the spring work. When he had spurred out from behind the bluff to turn the range horses, he had seen the head and neck of Mustang as he stood in the brush along the slough. As Sam looked his eyes were wide with surprise and delight. He saw Mustang standing there on the open place and he at once recognized him. He said aloud to himself, "It's Mustang! Sure as the world. Now ain't he a beauty! There he is and here we are. But with our horses just about played out from rounding up these range horses, no use to run him *now*. He'd run away from us easy."

Sam stood behind the bush, holding the reins of his puffing horse. Pretty soon two other men rode up behind Sam and then two more. One said, "What you looking at, Sam? We got all the horses. Got 'em all."

Jim Parkman and Bud Allen were among these men here. When they saw what Sam was looking at, instantly both exclaimed, "Mustang!" and Bud said, "Daggone his hide! Now *ain't* he the purtiest horse you ever laid eyes on!"

Mustang stood out in plain sight looking toward the bush and now he could see all the men and their horses as they moved out in the open and looked at him. After a moment Mustang whirled, kicked up his heels and galloped along the plain, keeping near the slough.

Sam, Jim and Bud watched him until he disappeared in a deep bend in the bluffs to the north. Jim said, "Well, Sam, at least there Mustang is and he's as big as life. What would you give for him in the stable?" There was a little silence, then Sam said, "Well, I got plenty of cattle and I'll give one thousand dollars for Mustang if he's brought to me in good shape. I don't want any man to try to crease him."

Jim grinned and said, "That ought to get him. If we can get him with our outfit, of course, he's free to you, but it may take several outfits. And now we'll get the word of your offer over to the Almazan Ranch and to the Buffalo Springs outfit and to the fellers up on the Shimmerhorn, and likely among us all we can run him down. My guess is that with all the outfits running him you'll have him and be scratching his neck in less than two weeks!"

X

THE men on the Almazan Ranch learned of the one-thousand-dollar reward for Mustang and they were the first to try to run him down. A rider on the Almazan one day saw Mustang grazing on the plains near what was known as the Sioux Bottoms. The next day the riders were out in force to attempt to run down the beautiful bay horse with the white stocking legs and black, flowing mane and tail.

The cowboys on the Almazan, twenty-five of them, were among the best of riders, and they were also skillful with their ropes. The horses they rode on this day were the pick of their range stock. The men tried the simple plan of having a dozen riders hide to the west of the Sioux Bottoms while other riders were concealed well to the northwest where they might ride out after Mustang when he had been run for miles by the men who started after him first. This plan of catching a swift horse like Mustang, though simple, was the hardest way, but it was also the quickest way if it succeeded.

The men rode out in the open and, by good luck, they were within a mile of Mustang when he saw them. They pushed him hard from the start and he, unknowing, ran on in the direction they desired him to run. He ran, mile after mile, easily keeping far ahead of the oncoming horsemen and running with no thought of anything but to keep going until his pursuers gave up. On and on, and still on, these persistent men came until many miles of the Sioux Bottoms had been crossed. The pace had been hard from the start and the horses the men rode

were puffing heavily when they reached the
end of the flats near a rise of ground. All at
once Mustang was amazed to see several
other men on horses dash out toward him
from a grove of trees on his left. So quickly
did they come that they were close when he
saw them, but he whirled and ducked his
head as a loop from a rope shot out toward
him, and again he leaped away and ran.

The men on fresh horses took up the chase
and rode desperately to catch up with him,
but hard pressed though he was, he gathered
his powerful muscles and ran with a burst of
speed that astonished the men. And urge
their horses as they would, the magnificent
bay horse steadily drew away from them and
at last, in the distance, they saw him disappear in the blue haze of the timbered hills
far to the west.

A week later a rider from the Almazan
stopped at the Horseshoe Ranch and told
Sam what had happened. The rider added,

"The fellers over on the Big Springs Ranch thought they'd like that one thousand dollars, Sam, and they tried to run Mustang down, too. One of their riders told us how it was. They knew where he was grazing and the whole outfit turned out the next morning. They found him in the middle of the forenoon. They had fellers stationed miles away and these waited on fresh horses. Things looked pretty good to the fellers on the Big Springs Ranch, for Mustang headed off in the direction they wanted him to run. About the time the first horses was tired out the ones on the fresh horses cut in and they pushed him for all they was worth and these run him until their horses was run down, then three other fellers on fresh horses rode after Mustang but he uncorked more speed and run out of sight among the ridges over toward the Shimmerhorn. The feller said he thought you sure had a thousand-dollar horse in Mustang, but he says the fellers at the Big

Springs think as we do that you ain't likely to get him because he's free and he aims to stay free. They understand you don't want any feller to try to crease him and they promised not to try that."

MUSTANG   191

XI

FROM the Almazan to the Big Springs, and from the Sioux Bottoms to the Shimmerhorn Ranch, the name of Mustang had become famous and several facts about him were known to all at this time. The cattlemen over this vast region knew that Mustang belonged to Sam McSwain, and they knew Sam offered one thousand dollars to the man, or men, who would capture Mustang and bring him in without doing him harm. They knew, also, that Mustang, with his bright bay coat and white stocking legs, was an extremely beautiful horse.

There was another fact about Mustang that was not generally known. This was that a few times he had been seen grazing with an old horse from the Horseshoe Ranch, a horse owned, also, by Sam.

This horse was Old Bill. Although he was getting on in years he was still tough, and when he came back to the stables of his own accord in the summer, Sam used to ride him a little. At such times Sam would put the saddle on Old Bill, scratch his neck and say to him, "Well, Bill, here you are again. You just have to come home to have me set up on your back. You're saying by this that you want to be with me again. That's fine. We'll go out for a little ride but not far and I'll turn you loose again. You've sure been a fine horse. I only wish you could find Mustang and get him to come in with you."

Old Bill was given a bucket of oats in his feed box and there was always a stall in the stable for him when he should come in. So it was that Old Bill was a privileged character. Sometimes, since Mustang had gone, he would be out on the range in the summertime for a whole month. Then he would suddenly come trotting, or galloping, in to the ranch. He could not forget Sam, for he had ridden Old Bill on the range for years, and it was Sam who had decided that the old horse should take things easy.

Mustang had known Old Bill well and there was no doubt whatever that these two remembered each other when they again met one day on a plain far to the west of the Horseshoe Ranch. Some of the men on the Shimmerhorn saw them together on two different occasions. Finally, it became known to all at the Shimmerhorn that Mustang was in the vicinity of their ranch. After the men had all decided to watch for him, they found that he was grazing on a grassy plain near the Shimmerhorn River. They believed he might remain there for some time since he had found very good grass not far from the river.

One day Dave Wilson, a top rider from the Shimmerhorn Ranch, saw Mustang feeding on this open plain near some wild horses. When Dave saw that Mustang was a little to one side, and by himself, he stopped his horse instantly and, under cover of a clump of trees, he watched the horses unseen. There was a big brown-colored stallion with the herd of wild ones, grazing out a little in front of the horses, and Dave wondered if Mustang was keeping his distance because he was afraid of the stallion. As he looked he found out. The stallion lifted his head a few times to look about for enemies, and all at once he started walking toward Mustang. The experienced Dave, who knew the ways of wild horses, noticed that the stallion did not run at Mustang, and by this he wondered if the stallion had had a tilt with Mustang before and so decided to be careful here.

Mustang went on grazing for a time as if he did not notice the stallion, but he suddenly jerked up his head, chewed on the grass he had in his mouth, and looked. The stallion kept coming on. All at once Mustang, with ears laid back, charged him. The stallion stopped, snorted, laid back his ears and, with head and nose straight out, his teeth showing, he moved forward. Mustang met him and charged face to face. Neither got his teeth on the other, but Mustang whirled and let fly both his hind hoofs, striking the stallion fair in the ribs. He kicked him again, whirled, shot in and grabbed the stallion by the flank.

The wild stallion tried to turn, but Mustang held on and while the stallion kicked back, hitting nothing but the air, Mustang bit him hard, "aiming to get enough for a mess," as the cowboys would have said. And when the stallion jerked free he *ran*. Mustang did not chase him. He stood spitting the hair from his mouth by rolling out his tongue, and he looked at the stallion as he ran in a wide circle to the rear of the other horses where he stopped, looked at Mustang, and snorted. Dave grinned and said under his breath, "That daggoned stud is saying to Mustang, 'Of course, if *that's* the way you feel about it, I'm plumb through with you! You got 'bout the worst temper of any horse I've ever met up with!' "

Mustang let out one tremendous snort. Dave grinned as he thought that Mustang must be thinking of the stallion, "That ain't the first time you've bothered me. And one of these times, if you don't stop it, I *may* get plumb mad and if I do the buzzards will have fresh stud meat for breakfast!"

Mustang went back to his grazing, and Dave watched with admiration. There he stood on the green plain, his beautiful bay coat shining in the sun, his white stocking legs looking whiter than ever. His body was tall, rangy, powerful. Such power in those great shoulders! They would thrill any cowboy to the depths. Dave looked with longing eyes. He had his rifle. Here might be a chance to crease him and so make him temporarily unconscious and capture him, but

Dave knew he might kill him, too. He thought to himself, "Nobody but a fool would try that on *him*. No feller that's got any sense would. But there's a chance to trap him or run him down. I'll wait."

Dave moved back and got quietly out of sight, and as he rode away from the place, he pondered on the plan already being worked out by the men on the Shimmerhorn Ranch to capture Mustang. The plan was to use an old wire trap corral built on the Shimmerhorn some years before to catch wild horses. The men would have to know where Mustang might be found, and Dave thought that Mustang might stay in this vicinity since the grass was good and it was as wild a place as the horses could find. Maybe Mustang would stay around long enough so that arrangements could be made for many riders from the Shimmerhorn to drive him toward the trap corral.

Dave rode home. That night he said to the men, "I saw Mustang today. He was with a bunch of wild ones. I saw him fight with the big wild stud that was out there and Mustang got plumb rough with that stud. He got his teeth in him and it looked like all at once Mustang had become a meat eater, and if that stud hadn't run, why, daggone my hide, I bet Mustang would have plumb chewed him up."

This made lively talk among the men. They enquired closely as to the lay of the land where Dave had seen Mustang, and after some conversation, it was agreed to allow Dave to watch a few days and see if Mustang had found a grazing ground where he might stay for a time. Then a day would be set to try to run him into the trap corral.

The next day Dave rode back to the locality and watched from the same point he had the day before. He saw the wild horses but they were farther away. Having his field glasses, Dave looked through them at the horses. He didn't need to look long to find that Mustang was not present. He lowered the glasses and said, "Well, he ain't there. Wonder where he's gone?"

As Dave rode away he kept a sharp lookout for Mustang. He hunted all that day and for three days following. On the evening of the last day he rode in at the ranch where a number of the men were lounging near the stables. The men looked at Dave expectantly as he rode up and one of them said, "Well, Dave, reckon you found out this time where Mustang is, didn't you?"

"No, I didn't," said Dave. "I didn't see hair nor hide of him. It's a queer thing, too. I saw another bunch of wild ones over on the Little Cottonwood, but Mustang wasn't with them. Along in the afternoon I thought for a minute I *did* see him. I was riding along at the foot of a ridge away out toward the Horseshoe Ranch when I got a glimpse of some horses in the cottonwoods near the river. I tied my horse to a tree and for a half hour worked my way on foot through the bushes until I got close enough to see, and I was plumb disgusted. What I had seen was that old broken down, bay range horse, Baldy, with his white stocking legs—him standing there with two other old plugs that nobody wants. I was up pretty close and that old range horse, Baldy, seen me. He had been about asleep when he raised his head and looked at me, as if he was saying to me, 'Well, Dave! It's nice to see you again! I didn't think you'd go to so much work getting through the brush just to come to see me! Awful nice of you to crawl a half hour through the brush to look at *me* again! I didn't know I was that popular!' And then he shut his eyes and went to sleep again. The other two didn't even wake up."

The men grinned. One of them said, "Well, Dave, what you going to do now?"

"*Do*," said Dave. "Not much, I guess. And I'll tell you about what'll happen. It'll be that Sam McSwain over on the Horseshoe will get Mustang if anybody does. And then Sam will have his horse and his thousand

dollars, too. Of course he's Sam's horse, anyway, but even if he wasn't I don't know of
anybody I'd rather see catch him than Sam
because Sam is a mighty fine young feller."

Every man agreed with Dave. One of
them said, "You bet Sam's a fine young
feller. Now if some fool Mexican don't try
to crease Mustang and so ruin him, maybe
Sam or some of us may get him."

All at once the men looked intently toward the west. Three riders were galloping
in. They rode up, their horses puffing and
their coats dark with sweat. Hank Bell, the
foreman, a tall, slim man, said as he and the
others dismounted, "We saw Mustang this
afternoon. He's living in that nice green
valley out between the Wild Horse Ridges."

All the men got to their feet. "And now,"
Hank went on, "we'll all start early tomorrow morning and I'll tell each feller where
to ride and hide. Why, that big bay Mustang
horse is in a natural trap there and don't
know it! He's grazing on the flats out there

that run for miles up to the west between the
two high ridges, and as you know, there's
that old trap for wild horses in the ravine
right at the end of the ridges. All we got to
do is to get ourselves placed right. I'll have
some of you ride out and hide behind the
ridges so that when we get Mustang running
to the west between the high ridges you can
show yourselves on top of the bluffs and
scare him back down on the level place in
between, and the rest of us will be running
him from behind. We'll just keep him running on between the ridges to the west and
after he's about run-down and our horses are
pushing him from behind he'll see the ravine
that leads up to the open highland beyond
and he'll think all he has to do is to run
through the ravine and on to the open spaces
and get away. And that's when he'll run
right into that wire trap. I don't see how he
can possibly break out, but to make certain,
two of you fellers can ride to the open spaces
on the high ground beyond the trap so you

can't be seen, and even if he should get out to the uplands, he'll be plumb run-down and two of you on fresh horses can ride right up close and throw your loops over his head. I think he'll fight us, though, because he shows he'll fight a stud or any kind of thing that attacks him, but he'll be so plumb tired out he can't do much."

They could not have picked a better place to try to capture Mustang than the one where the three men had seen him grazing late on this day. The question in all minds now was, "Would he still be in the same place the next day?"

The old trap corral, made of strong posts on which strands of barbed wire had been strung, had been made years before. It had been so well made, and the posts in the trap end of the corral so cleverly hidden among the leafy trees, that on one occasion a large number of wild horses had been driven into this trap and none of them escaped. They were roped and taken away for use on the range. Only a week before this, some of the men on the Shimmerhorn had looked at the trap and found the wires and posts in good condition. It seemed to the men that the trap was now more suitable for the purpose than ever since so long a time had gone by with nothing but natural growth around it.

To the men all seemed well for the capture of Mustang. It seemed to them that Nature, herself, had played into their hands. But Nature out here was a very uncertain thing, and while at times she played into the hands of the hunters, she was just as likely to deceive them and use her forces in the interest of the hunted. So it was that on this quiet evening when the men on the Shimmerhorn Ranch laid their plans to capture Mustang neither he nor they knew how freakish Nature might swing the result of this chase either way.

XII

THE riders of the Shimmerhorn Ranch rode forth the next morning a little after sunrise. There were, in all, thirty cowboys. All their plans had been made. One-third of the riders would first show themselves to the south of the Sioux Bottoms where there was a rolling country that would allow them to approach unseen. Then, far to the east and to the west of the Bottoms, where they could conceal themselves in clumps of trees, several riders would be waiting. And hidden behind the long, high ridges that led to the trap corral in the ravine were other riders. These last mentioned were ready to show themselves on top of the high ridges if Mustang tried to escape by running up the steep hills from the level plain below. Then, to make sure of their prize, the boss of the outfit had stationed two of the best riders in a low place on the highland near the head of the ravine. These two riders were mounted on swift horses. It was believed by all the men that if Mustang could be "pushed hard," as they said, for some fifteen miles back on the Sioux Bottoms, he would be so tired when he got in the trap corral that even if he should break out of it, the two cowboys on the fast horses there would be able to get close enough to throw their loops over his head.

As the men rode along in the early morning they talked and laughed together and most of their talk was good-natured banter as to how they would spend the one thousand dollars they would get from Sam McSwain for catching his great bay horse.

They kept to the low places in the rolling country as they approached the south end of the Sioux Bottoms, where they expected to find Mustang. Then, one of them stole forward for a peep over a high knoll with his field glasses. Almost at once he came hurrying back and said, "He's there! And he's grazing all alone! Not another horse to be seen anywhere!"

There was brief lively talk and the riders were then sent to their several stations. It would take quite some time for the men to get behind the ridges that could be seen in the distance. They must circle wide and so far away that Mustang might not see them at all, or if he did, he would pay little attention at such distance.

After a long time had passed the boss saw, with his field glasses, that the riders had gotten to their places. And now he and the men here, riding well apart, rode boldly up a ridge and down on the flats. There was no wind to warn Mustang, and with his head to the north he went on grazing for a short while before he saw the riders. Suddenly he threw up his head and looked at them. He stood for a time, his head high, looking. Then, with a snort, he galloped away, not swiftly but with long, easy bounds that seemed to him to be more than enough to escape those men at his rear. The men started after him and they held to a steady gallop which they knew the hardy range horses could continue for a long time before they would tire out.

On and on Mustang galloped. One of the men remarked, "Now ain't he a beauty! I don't blame Sam for offering a thousand dollars for that horse! And the chances look pretty good that we'll turn him over to Sam at the end of this race!"

That regular, unceasing gallop of the tough, wiry horses carrying the men continued for an hour. The horses' nostrils were dilated with their exertion and their coats were wet with sweat, but these horses were still able to gallop on and on. Another hour passed and now the horses, under the weight of the men, were breathing harder. Mustang

too was sweating and he felt some concern.
The men were still coming behind him, all
riding well apart. Mustang decided to shake
them off. He veered to the west, but he had
not run a hundred yards when a man rode
out from behind a small grove of trees in
that direction.

Mustang snorted, whirled back and ran
more rapidly to the north. The men riding
behind him urged their horses harder. A few
miles farther on, and again Mustang tried to
turn, this time toward the east. As he started
in that direction he was surprised and
troubled when suddenly a man on a horse
rode up from a depression. Mustang whirled
and ran hard. He was now running on the
level ground between the two high ridges
and he could see the long, level plain ahead
between the steep bluffs. It seemed to him he
could run straight on and outrun his pursuers, but when he looked back those persistent riders were still coming on, although
he was now getting ahead.

To Mustang men were creatures of strange power. They seemed small and weak when he looked at them yet they held a power that, even though he was free on the plain here, made him feel afraid. He could not think and plan as they could. All he knew was that he must run, just run and try to keep away from the men. Once they got those queer things over his head he would be caught. All he could do was to run and run and run. That was as far as he could plan things. And now he was running on the plain between the two high ridges. He thought he would like to get to a place where the men could not see him. All at once he had a desire to leap up the high ridge on the west where, it seemed to him, he would be rid of those men coming on so persistently. He leaped to the left and started plunging up the steep slope. It was hard going up a steep hill like this and he felt the exertion.

The men were gaining on him now but he thought that when he got to the top of the bluffs he would get away. He felt that the men could not see him then. But he was suddenly amazed when a man on a horse appeared on top of the ridge. At the same time, the man let out a yell. In terror Mustang ran down the hill at an angle. He reached the level again and the men below were nearer still so that he ran very fast.

After running hard for a time Mustang looked toward the ridge on the other side. But he did not even start up the slope for when he got to the base of it he saw a man on horseback at the top. With a little groan of terror he ran on straight ahead. He did not look now. He knew there was no use. The riders were still coming on and he knew the men were ready and waiting for him somewhere behind the high ridges. What he feared most was that some of them might appear directly ahead of him, but there was no sign of life in that direction. Then he saw the little ravine ahead—the ravine with its

tall trees. The open highland was just beyond.

The sun shone bright upon the trees ahead
and they stood in silence as if waiting and
watching. The trees had almost a peaceful
look to Mustang and they seemed to be
friendly to him. He would run through the
ravine and on up to the highland. But were
men also waiting on the highland? He was
breathing hard now and his once beautiful
bay coat was covered with sweat and foam.
Only his white stocking legs still showed
their natural color. Mustang's great dark
eyes were wide and shining and there was
something in them that told of suffering.

He plunged into the ravine and, unknowing, into the trap corral. A man hidden in the
ravine was seen to run out and close the gate
behind Mustang. Then came the wild shouts
of the men in the rear, riding on their spent
horses. The men believed that they had him.

But something had happened here to the
upper end of this trap corral. Two days be-

fore a high wind had blown down a dead tree. The tree had fallen on the fence, breaking down the two topmost wires, leaving the two lower ones still on their posts. When Mustang got into the ravine he ran on to escape but was appalled when he saw the fence confronting him. As he turned, in desperation, to run along the fence, he saw the break where the dead tree had fallen. He cleared the two wires, floundered to his knees, but at once got up and rushed on to the highlands above. He heard the wild shouts of some of those riders who had galloped up from behind the ridges. They charged around toward him.

Mustang reached the highland and ran with amazing speed. The two cowboys waiting there on fresh horses rode hard toward him, swinging their ropes as they came. They just missed, one of their ropes grazing Mustang's ear and falling useless to the ground. The men on the fresh horses took up the chase, but to their amazement Mustang held his own with them. In the distance they saw the timbered region known as the Jackson Hills, and, although they urged their horses desperately, Mustang drew away from them rapidly and they saw him vanish in the sheltered recesses of the deep woods, wild gorges and steep ravines of the Jackson Hills. Slowly the riders, all of them, on their puffing horses, gathered on the highland. They dismounted to let the horses rest before starting home.

Mustang, in the meantime, had reached the friendly shelter of the trees. As he did so he splashed through a little water hole, but in his desperate fear he did not even think of water. Once in hiding, however, he turned and looked back. After a time he saw the riders going away and at last he saw them disappear in the distance. He dropped his head and closed his eyes, and stood heaving. He felt flashing pains in his chest, and there was a terrible burning thirst in his throat. Puffing hard he got out to the little water hole. In running through it his hoofs had made the water muddy but he did not notice the muddy water. He drank as if each breath might be his last. But he drank all of it and even licked the mud for more. Fortunately, there was not too much water here. He wanted more—much more. But he was too exhausted to hunt for more. As always happens when a horse drinks when famished for water, even a small amount makes him feel better. So now Mustang felt the burning in his throat eased. He stood puffing, while looking back toward the place where he had last seen the men.

At last the shades of night began to fall on the land and the trees around him. He moved back a little into the woods and in the deep stillness he lay down. At first he lay with his head up as he breathed from his exhaustion, but at last he felt more comfortable and he lay his head down on the ground and his weary eyelids closed in a fitful sleep. Presently the moon arose and looked serenely

down on hill and plain. The moonlight fil-
tered through the leafy trees and fell on
Mustang and it lay so still it seemed to be
asleep with him. Only the slow movement
of his foam-covered sides told that he was
alive and gently breathing.

XIII

EARLY November came, yet the days up to this time had been as mild as late spring, and the buffalo grass which cured on the ground was plentiful. Sam McSwain had heard that Mustang was living on the rich grass and keeping fat on it, and so was Old Bill, for he was still allowed to go or come as he pleased.

One day Sam rode out toward a point where he had recently seen Old Bill. To his delight, on this day, he saw Mustang and Old Bill grazing together! But when Sam was half a mile away Mustang looked up, saw him, whirled and ran off like a streak. But Old Bill, as usual, stood his ground, for he was not afraid. Sam rode up, dismounted, and gave Old Bill some biscuits, something the old horse had always been fond of. Sam put a rope on Old Bill, and mounting his horse, said, "Come on, Bill. We'll see if we can get Mustang to come to the ranch again like he used to do when you came in."

When Sam arrived at the ranch stable that day he told the men what he had seen. He said he hoped to see Mustang coming across the plain toward the ranch some night. The other men were divided in their opinions about the matter. Some thought Mustang might pay Old Bill a secret visit some night, some that Mustang had been too much scared to venture so close to men again. Certainly he had had to do some desperate running to escape them and Mustang had been a long time away from Sam.

But Sam guessed right. On the third night of his watch near the stable in which Old Bill was tied, Sam saw Mustang. It was a bright, moonlight night and the trees near

the stable stood in complete silence for there
was no wind stirring. The range horses, used
by the men, were in two corrals near the
stable. All these horses were being fed oats
and so was Old Bill who was now licking up
the last of his oats. Then he began to move
about in his stall. Sam, who was hidden in
the shadows of a clump of trees, could hear
him. After a long time Sam became sleepy
in the stillness, but suddenly he was wide
awake. He said afterwards that he must
actually have fallen asleep for when he
looked he saw the great rangy form of Mustang standing in the moonlight so near that
his white legs could be plainly seen.

Sam sat in the shadows with his back
against the trunk of a tree and he did not
move—just looked at Mustang. Mustang
stood for a time looking toward the ranch
house, flicking his ears back and forth in the
manner of a horse who is uncertain about
something near him. At this moment Old
Bill must have scented Mustang for he

whinnied softly but eagerly. At once Mustang walked up to the stable door and put his head inside the dark place. Old Bill could be heard stepping about in the stable and he now kept up a slow whinnying and plainly enough he was "talking" to Mustang. Mustang also made low whinnying sounds, and this went on for a brief time. But Mustang was afraid to do more than put his head inside the stable.

After a little while he walked away from the stable door and, moving up close to one of the corrals, he looked at the horses through the openings of the long poles. Snortings from the range horses greeted him, and they were the kind of snorts that told that the horses knew Mustang was a stranger. But this did not bother him. While Mustang stood here two large horses that had the run of the place walked up from where they had been standing behind the stable. One of them walked up close, made a friendly sound, then walked away. Mustang stood looking at the horse as he moved away, then Mustang went on with his investigation of the place. He spent some time looking at the horses inside both the big corrals, then he moved watchfully toward the house where it stood all dark and silent in the night.

After looking a little toward the house he walked back toward the stable where Old Bill was, and as he did so, he came close to the place where Sam sat in the shadows near the tree. Suddenly Mustang stopped not ten feet from him, and Sam was almost afraid to breathe. Mustang reached his head down toward the shadows and looked. Sam sat as still as a stone. Mustang raised his head, gave a snort, and then, poking his nose down toward Sam, he blew through his nostrils. Sam said afterwards that he believed it possible that Mustang remembered his scent, much as a dog would that had known a certain kindly human for several years.

In the meantime Old Bill could be heard stepping about in his stall in the stable and once he let out a nicker which plainly told Sam that Old Bill wanted to come out there where Mustang was and see what was going on. When Old Bill nickered Mustang stopped looking down at Sam in the shadows and walked over to the stable door. He looked inside at Old Bill and made low friendly sounds, then he walked back and peered into the shadows toward the motionless Sam.

Mustang again went to the stable, looked in and snorted. He seemed to be saying in cowboy talk, "I *would* come in and pay you a visit but there's a *feller* out there in the shadows—a feller that sets as still as a rock, but he can't fool me for I know he *is* a feller! And he *seems* like the wonderful feller I knowed a long time ago. But I'm not certain and I'm too scared to come inside!"

Mustang snorted, leaped back, kicked up his heels and ran around the place in a big circle. Once more he went up to the open doorway of the stable and looked in. Suddenly, with a frightened snort he whirled and ran away. This time he ran on and as Sam waited and listened in the shadows of the trees, he heard Mustang still running and now and then letting out a snort. He did not stop and the sounds of his hoof beats sounded farther and farther away. Old Bill knew that Mustang was running away and he let out two shrill, piercing nickers, trying to call him back.

XIV

THE next morning Sam told all the men what had happened. They were delighted. Jim Parkman said, "Sam, I bet you'll get that horse with little trouble. You always was the daggondest feller with horses. Especially when you've got biscuits."

"It's so," said the grizzled cook, Buck Jenkins, who stood at the end of the table pouring another cup of black coffee for Sam. "Sam takes 'bout half of my biscuits to feed the horses he rides."

Charley Malone said, "Well, Buck, fellers like biscuits. What's the difference between fellers and horses?"

"There ain't no difference," said Buck

with a grin, "except horses like Old Bill should have all the *good* biscuits and fellers should have all the *sour* ones!"

Charley grinned and said, "Of course." And strange though it might have seemed to a "tenderfoot," Charley and all these men actually meant that. A truly faithful horse, as Old Bill had been on the range, was cared for *first*. That's the kind of men these were.

On this morning, well along in November, Sam mounted Old Bill and rode away to find Mustang. He saw him within three miles of the ranch! He suddenly came upon him feeding alone at the foot of a low hill. Instantly Mustang threw up his head and looked, and at once Old Bill looked at Mustang and he nickered loud and earnestly. Then Old Bill started trotting toward Mustang and he nickered as he trotted. Mustang stood looking. He snorted, lifted his head and tail high, and trotted majestically around in a circle. He stopped and looked, and again snorted, but he didn't run away—just trotted around in a circle. Old Bill was now very near and again he nickered as Mustang moved away at a slow trot. Bill trotted, too, and nickered as if he were saying plainly, as a cowboy would have said, "Hello, there, Mustang! Daggone your hide—I'm glad to see you. Wait! Let's talk things over!" And Old Bill tried to come up. But Mustang trotted off a little way, stopped and snorted. Again and again Old Bill nickered, but Mustang trotted on. Old Bill tried to gallop and champed at his bit as Sam held him back.

Once Sam got near enough to Mustang to throw his rope, but he suddenly decided not to do this. He might miss with the rope. Then he thought of riding back home, letting the time go by and seeing if Mustang would come in of his own accord. But from what he had seen here, he decided to take a chance on something else. Mustang had come to the ranch that night where he knew Old Bill lived. Sam knew Mustang *wanted* to come up—wanted to come up to Old Bill and to Sam and stay in the stable where Old Bill was. But Sam knew that Mustang could not quite do that yet. And he knew the horse might get into trouble any day now. Winter might come on suddenly. All this went through Sam's mind. No, he would follow Mustang. It was a nice warm day and he would just let Old Bill go on and see if Mustang would at last stop.

Several miles were traveled and Mustang, as it happened, headed toward the north. He seemed to be having a grand time in it all. When Sam rode Old Bill up a long grassy slope, Mustang waited and Sam got so close to him he could see his dark eyes. Mustang lowered his head, let out a little squeal, kicked up his heels and galloped a little, then he again stopped and snorted and waited for Sam and Old Bill to come up within a few yards. Sam pulled Old Bill to a stop and said affectionately to Mustang, "Now, Mustang, daggone your ornery hide, you don't need to show *me* how fast you can run. I know already. What makes you go on and act this way? You act like a kid that's trying to plague some grown person. Just listen to Old Bill talking to you. Now ain't you ashamed!" And Old Bill *was* talking to Mustang. He was making the sounds that would tell any cowboy as plain as day that he "wanted Mustang to quit this daggone foolishness and act like a horse and not a fool colt!" But again Mustang lowered his head and squealed, and this time he galloped clear around Old Bill and Sam. As he galloped he took time to kick up his heels and then stop and look at them as if he were scared.

But Sam knew he was not much scared. Once when Mustang stopped and came close, Sam said, "I guess I know what you want. You want to coax me and Old Bill off some place where you'll never see fellers again. Then you think us three would have it fine. But we can't do that. If you'll come with Old Bill and me, we'll show you the kind of fellers that's the finest." Mustang snorted and pranced off again.

It was a time of the year when few riders were out on the ranges. Sam had not seen a man since he left the ranch earlier in the day. Noon came and passed. Mustang was so tantalizing that he took time to stop and eat of the buffalo grass now and then, and he seemed to be having a good time. But along in the middle of the afternoon he did something that Sam never forgot. Sam, like the other cowboys, when starting out on an all-day ride on the range, carried some hard biscuits. Strangely enough Sam had forgotten about the biscuits until now. Mustang had stopped and Old Bill was within a few feet of him. Sam held out a biscuit toward him. Mustang saw that biscuit and he also smelled it. Sam held it out and said, "Here, Mustang, come on up. I got a whole one and some more for you," and he held out the biscuit at arm's length. Mustang licked his lips as he came up. He gently took the biscuit from Sam's hand. Old Bill put his nose on Mustang and "talked" to him. Sam had a rope in his right hand, ready for this. He held another biscuit in his mouth and he slowly dismounted. But Mustang wasn't scared now. He began to beg for more biscuits. Sam held one in his left hand, and while Mustang nibbled at it Sam rubbed Mustang's neck with his other hand and at the same time eased the rope over the top of Mustang's neck so it hung down. Old Bill held his head toward Sam now, too, and he was trying to get biscuits. This helped. Sam reached under Mustang's neck and got the end of the rope and quietly tied it. The other end was tied to the saddle horn on Old Bill. But Mustang did not care and Sam knew that Mustang knew.

Sam was as happy as a boy. The time passed while he rubbed Mustang's neck and talked to him. When Mustang put his nose to Sam, Sam said to him, "I'm going to ride you home. Bill will follow." Leading them to a tree, Sam tied Mustang, took the saddle from Old Bill and put it on Mustang. Then Sam untied him, patted him on the neck and said, "Mustang, you wouldn't fight me, would you?" Mustang put his head down close to Sam and his eyes looked fine and gentle. Sam tied the rope on the saddle and mounted. They started toward the south. And Sam always believed that in Mustang's brain he had already decided that he wanted to go to the ranch where he knew Old Bill and Sam lived.

Sam had been so occupied with the situation that he had not even thought of the weather. He knew, as did every cattleman of the Old West, that when November came, any day or night winter might come. It might come on a mild day with a terrible wind and snow sweeping down from the north to freeze and kill any living thing in the open that could not quickly find shelter. And Sam, with the other men, knew that in the plains country the temperature on a mild day in November had been known to drop

forty degrees in a few minutes, when the
cold rushed down with one of these oncoming
storms. As Mustang moved along at an easy
gallop, with Old Bill following, a blast like
this now struck. Sam, amazed, turned in the
saddle and looked back. He saw a strange
darkness in the north. Mustang sensed the
danger. Sam did not have to touch him, for
he leaped away when the icy blast struck.

Old Bill, now free to do as he liked, did
the one thing that instinct told him to do—
he ran toward the south for home. For some
distance he ran behind Mustang and the two
of them thundered down the low level valley. Old Bill was a horse with average speed
and he was now running as hard as he could.
Sam felt the mighty power of Mustang
under him. He ran in long swift leaps, keeping ahead of Old Bill, and Sam knew this
great horse was running easily. Old Bill, in
his effort, stretched his head out, his nose almost even with his knees, but Mustang
leaped forward, his head up, his long black

mane tossing in the wind. As Sam looked at
Mustang he was sure he understood the danger sweeping down from the north upon
them.

When they reached a turn in the valley
toward the east Old Bill leaped across a dry
gully and headed out of the valley toward
some rough country that would offer a
shorter cut to the ranch. But Mustang did
not seem to notice what Old Bill had done.
He ran on down the level valley and followed at the foot of a high ridge leading
southeast, and this was what Sam wanted.
He knew that Old Bill's instinct was true
enough in that he was taking the shortest distance, but there was much rough land in that
course, rolling ground and sharp slopes and
ridges to be crossed. The valley trail was
longer but it was level and so a horse was not
so likely to stumble. Moreover, the ranch
stable was close to the edge of the valley,
just where the high ridge turned again to the
north. But Sam knew that in a blinding bliz-

zard nothing could be seen—not even the high ridge.

When Old Bill leaped the gully and struck out alone, Mustang ran forward with a burst of speed that astonished Sam, and he bowed low over the saddle horn. Here was a man of the Old West and his horse, with possible death roaring and steadily closing in from the rear. Yet even in the present danger he was thrilled at this magnificent horse. Thoughts raced through Sam's brain like lightning. No wonder the best riders of the ranches with all their best horses had not been able to catch Mustang. No wonder that the owner of the Shimmerhorn Ranch had said he would pay Sam fifteen hundred dollars for Mustang if someone could catch him and Sam would sell him.

Another icy blast struck that chilled Sam to the bone, and he slapped Mustang's mighty shoulder and said, "Let's go, Mustang, we'll fight it out together!" Mustang leaped yet faster to the touch and he was eating up the distance as he ran, but the appalling blizzard was coming faster still.

Down the level valley they raced, with Sam leaning low, his face buried in Mustang's mane. Sam thought of everything now. Immediately ahead the low valley curved toward the east from where it led on and on to the ranch with nothing to bother, except a few low bushes far down. As Mustang leaped on with mighty bounds he edged close to the low hill on the left of the valley, and having come close to the hill he raced along near the base of it. Sam knew this ridge dropped away to the level ground just where the ranch stable and house stood. When Mustang did this Sam wondered, "Did Mustang do this to give himself a guide to the stable when the awful storm should strike?" Sam did not know but he believed Mustang did this to keep near the base of the hill and so not miss the ranch. Then for once, and once only, the thought flashed through Sam's brain that when the blizzard struck with all its force Mustang might become so frightened and confused that he would forget everything and so lose his head and run past the ranch. "Maybe," Sam thought, "I have made an awful mistake to take the saddle from Old Bill and put it on Mustang! Old Bill was always so dependable. If I had stayed on Old Bill the old horse would have kept on fighting to get to the ranch." But his miserable doubt passed quickly. He trusted this horse under him. To Sam in all this there was a trust in Mustang much like the trust of one fine man in another when death threatens them both.

Now the blizzard with all its fury struck Sam and Mustang, and the icy wind bit deep, for it was below zero. And, unbelievable as it would seem to those who never knew these storms of the West, the day suddenly turned to night. The rushing, roaring, howling wind and snow gripped and tore at Sam and Mustang, trying to freeze them, to blind them, to choke them with this deadly seething mass.

Trained son of the Old West that Sam was, he leaned low and held on to Mustang. There was no use now to wish he had stayed on Old Bill, no use to do anything but to hug this mighty horse and trust him. If it had not been that death itself was so near Sam might have known that already his ears and his fingers were freezing, but in the face of impending death, a man does not feel pain—the mind only is supreme.

The roar of the storm, with its blinding snow, the cold cutting like a knife, was appalling. It was so dark that Sam could see nothing as he bent his head low against the neck of Mustang. Surely now, Sam thought, Mustang would have to run blind. No living thing could see anything in all this. But could there be a smell to guide Mustang when he ran close to the ranch? Smell, that strange, wild thing of animals that is above the power of man to know—that might

make this horse *know* when it was time to
turn and so reach the stable. Sam knew it was
some fifty yards from where the hill turned,
but Mustang would have to face the storm
those fifty yards to reach the stable. He held
his right hand down on the shoulder of Mustang. He was conscious of mighty muscles
moving there and he knew Mustang was running hard. It seemed a thousand thoughts
rushed through Sam's brain. If Mustang
should stumble and fall and Sam were
thrown off—he would be lost, for he could
not see Mustang three feet away, nor could
Mustang see him. Sam thought it would be
impossible in all this for Mustang to think
about the stables and where to turn. It seemed
that it would be expecting too much of him.
He might rush on and on like the average
horse, caught in these wild, deadly blizzards,
that runs on until he falls exhausted and
there gives up and dies in the storm.

Old Bill again flashed into Sam's mind.
The old horse had taken a shorter cut across

the hills. Was he already home and even now in the snug stable, safe from this awful thing? If Mustang ran on down the valley and missed the stable, when could he possibly stumble into a place where he and Sam might at least find a crude shelter? Sam remembered that far down the valley there was a thin belt of willows and cottonwoods along a small stream. But such shelter was a mockery. And the men at the ranch? Were Charley and Jim and Bud and all the others there? Sam felt sure they were, for when he had left the ranch that morning they had no special work to do. In any case there was little cause for any of them to ride far out on the range at this season of the year.

Suddenly Mustang stumbled to his knees and Sam gripped his neck at the shock, but Mustang was up on his feet again instantly and he rushed on. All at once Sam felt something brushing hard against his boots in the stirrups and he knew Mustang was running through a patch of low brush. Sam remem-

bered that there was a clump of low bushes
down the valley less than a mile on this side
of the ranch house, but he knew, also, that
there was a clump of low bushes *beyond* the
ranch! Had Mustang missed the ranch and
was he running now through the low thickets
farther down the valley, and just running on
and on, he knew not where? Sam did not
know. But it seemed that possibly everything
had gone wrong. After all, how could Mustang know anything in all this howling fury?
Lying low with his face against Mustang's
mane, another thought flashed through Sam's
mind. He felt a numbness in his hands and
feet, and he remembered that several winters
before a cowboy had been caught out in a
blizzard and the horse he rode had done all
any horse could do; he ran true as to direction and he reached the ranch stable, and the
cowboy, numbed and unconscious, tumbled
from the saddle to the ground. The next
morning the men had found him dead in a
snowdrift not far from the stable. In this ter-

rific cold Sam felt the numbness creeping over him. And he felt the brush drag against his boots in the stirrups. He was sure he must know soon whether it was to be life or death.

The time, to Sam, seemed so long. Surely, he thought, Mustang must have passed the ranch and surely he must be running, wild and panic-stricken, before the storm, just running as panic-stricken cattle did. Again Sam thought of possible shelter that Mustang might stumble into, but he knew there was none if he had passed the ranch—nothing but that pitifully thin belt of small willows and cottonwoods along the stream.

All at once Sam realized that Mustang had turned—turned sharply—and now he was plunging directly into the face of this freezing, blinding thing. Sam gasped for breath in the smother of the driving snow. The thought flashed happily in his mind that Mustang had turned at the right place—he had turned where the ridge turned sharply and where that big ranch stable was—hardly fifty yards away. That distance was short but Mustang had to fight for it.

Then suddenly Mustang stopped and Sam was aware of a lull in the terrific wind. Somehow he got off Mustang's back to the ground. His numb hands touched the side of the stable, he heard human voices, and the next second he stumbled inside the big stable. Mustang followed. All at once three men were around Sam. They were Jim Parkman, Charley Malone and Bud Allen. They were all talking to Sam at the same time. Jim rubbed the snow from Sam's face with his big red handkerchief while Sam leaned against a stall and breathed hard. By the aid of a lighted lantern Jim and Charley and Bud saw that it was *Mustang* that had brought Sam in. How Sam got him and how it happened that Old Bill was not here were things that must wait. Jim felt of Sam's ears and of Sam's fingers, then said, "Sam, your ears and the ends of your fingers are froze and I reckon there'll be frostbites in your toes, too, but otherwise you seem to be all in one piece."

Sam drew a long breath, like a tired horse that at last gets his breath. He went into the stall where Mustang was. Charley had taken the saddle and bridle off so Mustang would feel easy. Mustang turned his head around to Sam. Sam put his hands up on Mustang's head and Mustang held his head quiet, breathing hard. And Sam's body shook a little as he held his hands on that horse's head, but it wasn't the cold that made Sam quiver. There was no sound from him. These men didn't talk at a time like this. They *couldn't.* The lantern, hanging on a wooden peg behind the stall, shone on the men and on Mustang standing there. No word was said. Sam patted Mustang a little on the neck, then finally said, "Let's give him some oats."

Charley put the oats in Mustang's feed box and Mustang began to eat. He showed no fear at all while Charley and Bud carefully brushed the snow from him. Jim meanwhile was putting snow on Sam's frostbitten ears and fingers, "to help thaw him out some."

The blizzard outside was roaring. A long rope had been stretched from the house to the stable, a common practice in these blizzards. After some time all the men, by the aid of this rope, started out and Jim kept a tight grip on Sam's wrist while they went through that blinding storm to the house.

These blizzards of the West usually lasted from one to three days. This one was of short duration. It roared through the night, but morning came with a bright sun shining. All the men then went out to the stable. Sam went in first and talked to Mustang. He gave him his oats and rubbed him while Mustang ate. Sam's ears and fingers and his toes were sore, but he paid no attention. These men here were not the kind that paid attention to such things.

The time passed quickly. It was the middle of the afternoon. Perhaps nowhere in the world is the weather more freakish than out here in the West. By noon the sun shone actually warm. The snow was melting and water was dripping from the eaves of the stable. Sam had Mustang outside, tied to a post, and with currycomb and brush he was making Mustang's bay coat fairly shine in the sun while all the men of the ranch, with admiring eyes, stood looking on.

Suddenly Charley looked out on the snow-covered ground to the north and said, "Well, daggone my hide! If there don't come Old Bill!"

And it was so. What shelter he had found was never known, but here he was, and when he reached some bare ground where the snow had been blown away, he came galloping up, ran into the stable and right up to his feed box. There he turned, looked at the men, snorted, licked the bottom of his feed box and looked again at the men. Charley put some oats in Old Bill's feed box and, as he did so, Sam, who stood looking in, said, "Old Bill's

saying to us, 'Don't stand and gawk at me—
give me my oats!'"

While Sam resumed his brushing of Mustang's bright coat, Jim looked Old Bill over.
Shortly, Jim came outside where Sam was and
said, "Old Bill's all right except that the
tops of his ears is froze. The tips will come
off but that's all. He'll look like a daggone
timber wolf but he won't care!"

"That's so," said Charley. "Old Bill's the
most unparticular horse that way, we've ever
owned."

While all the men stood looking on, Sam
kept on with his work of brushing Mustang.
The time went by, and Jim said, "Sam, if you
don't quit you'll have Mustang's coat so daggone shiny it'll hurt a feller's eyes to look at
him."

But Sam said nothing. He only grinned,
and he just kept on brushing.